My Little Trainwreck

Eric Moyer

My Little Trainwreck is the first book in the Laura Summer Series!

Subscribe to the newsletter to receive news on upcoming books in the series, as well as sneak peeks, free book downloads and bonus chapters only available to subscribers!
www.mylittletrainwreck.com/newsletter.html

Download the author's first book:
Back to Ocean City:
A Screenwriter's Journey
featuring the original movie script for
My Little Trainwreck.
www.amazon.com/gp/product/B00X3C7348

Cover Inspiration/Website Model
Brooke Ashlynn Miller
www.brookeashlynnmiller.com
Special Thanks:
Travis Skidmore and Megan Miller

Book Cover Design by
The Scarlett Rugers Book Design Agency
www.booksat.scarlettrugers.com

TABLE OF CONTENTS

CHAPTER ONE
Childhood's End

She was once America's little girl. *My Little Robot* was the number one television show in the country. Everyone watched it on Thursday nights. It was the kind of show that reminded you of *The Brady Bunch*. In fact, the father on the show looked just like a thirty-something Greg Brady. But he wasn't the star. The show belonged to Laura Summer. When it aired, she was only five years old and became a bona fide television and movie star.

Magazine covers. Talk shows. Awards. She even had a star on the Hollywood Walk of Fame by the age of ten, but like most child stars, she never recaptured that magic and struggled to get film and television roles as she got older.

Instead, she dated famous actors and got caught up in the Hollywood nightlife. She was photographed dancing on tables, falling over drunk and panty-less getting out of cars. She got into bar fights, posed for countless mugshots and entered her twenties a tabloid fixture.

At age twenty-two, Laura's attempt at a comeback began on a first-class flight with her mother from Los Angeles to Philadelphia. Sophia Summer was a slinky, and very sexy woman, even in her fifties. Heavy makeup and years of plastic surgery paid off. They were mother and daughter, but Sophia looked so young, they could pass for sisters.

As Laura and Sophia each read through copies of the movie script for *Pretty Ugly*, neither one could contain their excitement. This was the first time they were reading it. It was a top secret script and Laura blindly accepted the part just to work with the director, Jimmy Corn.

"Mom, this is really good," Laura gushed.

Sophia agreed. "This is a wonderful move for you dear. A revelation, a showcase role."

Laura smiled ear to ear and laughed to herself as she flipped through the pages. This was the script she had been waiting for. Her return to the A-list. It was happening. She could feel it. She knew this script was her chance to shake her tabloid image as a "trainwreck."

After their plane landed, Laura and Sophia waited patiently at baggage claim. Laura waved her hand to clear the air. She sniffed and looked directly at Sophia. "Mother, what is that perfume you're wearing?"

"It's a new fragrance. I got it in a gift bag last week."

"I love it. Can you get me a bottle?" asked Laura.

Their conversation was interrupted when a random woman tapped Laura on the shoulder.

"Are you Laura Summer?"

She replied with a very matter-of-fact, "Yes."

"Can I get a picture with you?"

Sophia whispered into Laura's ear. "Your fan base, dear."

Laura was so focused on her new project that any unwanted attention was a nuisance to her. She reluctantly put on a fake smile. "Sure."

The woman leaned her head into Laura and held a camera out in front of them.

Before she snapped a picture, she told Laura, "I loved *My Little Robot*."

On the show, Laura portrayed T.A.R.A., which stood for Technologically Advanced Robotic Adolescent. Her character was a robot in the form of a child, complete with flashing lights and dangling wires.

The fan confessed, "I used to torture my parents with your robot dance."

Those last two words made Laura's lips curl into a snarl just as the picture was taken. The woman moved on, but Laura was stunned from the combination of the camera flash and the dreaded reminder of the robot dance.

As popular as the robot dance was, Laura got sick at the mere thought or mention of it. She wanted the fans to remember her for her performance as T.A.R.A., not for the robot dance.

Once they had their luggage, they continued through the airport. Sophia handed a checklist to Laura. "Rehearsal and a radio show on Thursday. Hotel, directions, rental car over there. I'm taking a cab to meet Victor for dinner. Ta-ta."

"But Mom..."

Sophia planted a goodbye kiss on Laura's cheek. "You'll be fine. I love you, angel."

Laura waved back as Sophia hurried off.

While Sophia was no longer married to Laura's father, Seymour Summer, she remained very hands-on with Laura's career and served as her manager. This was probably a mistake, as Laura needed someone to be tough on her. Instead, Sophia spoiled her just like she did when she was a kid.

Most people didn't know Laura's father was the television producer behind *My Little Robot*. After the series ended, Laura didn't work again until her father cast her in the hit show *Venice*

Beach, 90291, and even then, the real star was her brother, Ricky Summer.

Sophia disappeared into a cab and Laura stood there all alone and watched her drive away. She was a bit frightened. This was a big moment for her and she was out of her comfort zone so far away from Los Angeles. But that all changed once she picked up her expensive rental car and put the top down. She typed an address into the GPS, turned the music up and let the wind take her long blonde hair.

Laura danced in the driver's seat while slapping the steering wheel to the beat of the music. She squinted her eyes just to read the road signs and missed lots of turns. The GPS continuously said, "Re-routing." Other cars beeped their horns at her as she made reckless U-turns.

Laura turned down the music when she heard her cell phone ringing. The screen said the incoming call was from her much older boyfriend, action star Tony Steel. Dating Tony was a desperate attempt to change her image and it had worked. The public had a bizarre fascination with the unorthodox couple. You couldn't walk by a magazine rack without seeing them on the cover of a tabloid.

Laura answered the phone with a generic, "Hello?"

Tony's obnoxious voice blasted through the phone. "Hey, baby doll."

"Hi, Tony," Laura continued in her monotone voice.

Tony Steel started his career as a Krav Maga instructor for the stars. Krav Maga was a self-defense system used by the Israeli military. In Hebrew, it translated to 'contact combat'. While it discouraged confrontation, if a fight was necessary, the method called for the quickest and most efficient finish, which sometimes involved attacking the eyes, knees, groin and other sensitive areas. Legend had it Tony was responsible for the artificial eye of a certain A-list actor in Hollywood who made a pass at one of his girlfriends at a party.

"There's been a change of plans. I'm on a plane to Budapest."

"Budapest?! Does that mean you're not coming here?" Laura had to hide her excitement. While a break-up seemed imminent, they had both managed to keep their relationship together by a thread.

Tony continued, "They want me for *On Bloody Ground Part 3*."

"But you weren't even in *Part 2*!"

"That's why I'm in *Part 3*, because the guy in *Part 2* sucked."

Laura already had zero interest in the phone conversation before hearing about this. Just when it seemed Tony couldn't sign up for a more ridiculous film role, he always surprised her with another one. Besides, Laura knew her career was on the upswing. It was time for her to move on from Tony Steel.

"Sorry I'm going to miss your birthday, unless you want to fly to Budapest."

Laura had heard enough. "Bye, Tony."

Tony yelled through the phone, "Don't you hang..." *Click*. The sudden change of tone in Tony's voice sent shivers through her. As they grew apart, Tony became verbally abusive toward Laura, and sometimes even got physical with her. As much as she wanted to break up with him, there was a part of her that was afraid to do it. She hoped he would get the hint and just do it himself. With Tony in Budapest, it put some much needed distance between them, and Laura preferred to keep it that way. Most of Hollywood was afraid of him, and no producers wanted Tony Steel anywhere near their film set.

Tony's first film, *Torpedo Man*, was a massive hit, but a series of flops led to straight-to-video movies that often featured his name in the title, like *Steel Vengeance* and *Born to Steel*. There were even rumors of a film Tony and Laura shot together set on a deserted island called *Steel Summer*. Word on the street was the film was so bad it was unreleasable. Tony and Laura were a paparazzi's dream.

~ * ~

Victor's Bar and Grill wasn't the nicest bar in the area, but it wasn't a dive either. It was sandwiched between a hardware store and a barbershop on a well-lit street in a quiet neighborhood. The sign outside that flashed the name of the bar needed some bulbs and the interior had its share of broken bar stools, missing floor tiles and faded paint. Sure, it could have used a modern facelift, but the locals were fond of its lived-in look. All the customers knew each other and this was the place to go and vent after a long day at work, an argument at home or simply to enjoy a cold beer.

When you walked in, you were greeted with a homemade sign above the bar that announced, "Welcome Shannon Green." Another sign read, "Welcome Cast and Crew of *Pretty Ugly*."

It wasn't the busiest place. The regulars were there all day, but there were always some seats available. Never any real trouble. Just the random fight here and there—typical for any bar.

Scott Simmons walked in with a stack of fliers and a roll of tape. He was the manager and sported a 'staff' shirt. Scott was about as average as a guy could be with a short haircut and some facial scruff. Not a bad looking guy, but he wasn't a model or bodybuilder either.

He headed straight to the corner of the bar where a well-dressed man in his fifties, Dennis, flipped through a newspaper. When he saw Scott coming, he looked at his watch and greeted him with, "You're early."

Scott immediately responded, "It's my last day as an employee."

Dennis shook his head. "Trust me, you have no idea how much work owning a bar really is."

Dennis didn't have kids of his own, so Scott always felt he was treated like a son. He knew that Dennis turned down many lucrative offers to give him a fair chance to buy the bar at a reasonable price, even though he really needed the money. Dennis accumulated various debts over the years that only Scott knew about.

"Just be thankful I gave you first crack at buying it," Dennis reminded him.

For Scott, this was the opportunity of a lifetime. Owning a bar in your twenties didn't happen to many people. It wasn't a done deal though. In addition to all his savings, Scott was depending on some financing from the bank.

"The loan is a lock."

"Hope you get it," Dennis replied.

Scott sensed nervousness in Dennis' answer and insisted, "Nothing to worry about." Indeed, Scott was overconfident in his finances and was heavily relying on the loan from the bank to cover the amount he was short. Without that extra money, the deal would completely fall apart, but in Scott's mind, that couldn't possibly happen. He didn't have a back-up plan.

Scott slammed the bar with his hand. "Where's my bartender?"

Alison rushed out from the back room and quickly poured him a glass of water. Alison was a twenty-something, Goth girl with dark hair and heavy black makeup. She was always cute, but once she started with the makeup, she got carried away, and Scott sometimes felt like she was hiding behind a mask.

Scott pointed right at her. "I'm going to need a new manager. You got what it takes?"

Alison reminded him of her qualifications, "I practically manage your house and your life. I can handle your bar. Just make sure I get a part in this movie." Scott was her big brother, and as much as he protected her over the years, she equally looked out for him.

Scott returned his attention to the stack of fliers and taped one to the wall behind his bar stool. It read, "Be an Extra in *Pretty Ugly*. See Scott for Details." He moved a few feet down and hung another flier. Then another. And another. In minutes, the entire bar was plastered with fliers about how to become a movie extra.

Scott boasted, "I'm telling you, *Pretty Ugly* is going to turn this place into a local tourist attraction." Not only was Scott certain he was getting the loan, he sincerely believed that once he owned it, the celebrity factor would turn it into the hottest destination on the East Coast. He envisioned crowds of people lined up outside, guest lists and reservations for tables. Scott was always a dreamer.

Dennis kept him in check once again. "As long as it's a good movie."

"With Jimmy Corn directing? Are you kidding? It'll be an instant classic."

Jimmy Corn blazed onto the scene with his independent film *River Cats*, which he shot in black-and-white with his friends cast in the lead roles. It was a gut-wrenching story of two competing video stores in a small town whose clerks took their rivalry a little too far. Despite the blood and gore, the public ate it up and Jimmy Corn became the next big thing.

Dennis was confused and gave Scott a disgusted look as if he just saw something horrific. "There's just one thing I don't understand. Jimmy Corn makes all those violent action flicks, right?"

Scott defended Jimmy Corn the only way he knew how. "*Blunt Drama* is one of the greatest movies of all time."

Dennis continued to grill Scott about Jimmy. "Then why is he making a romantic comedy?"

Pretty Ugly was strategically chosen by his handlers as the next project to show off the brand new, kinder and gentler Jimmy Corn. The box office predictions were soft though, so he wasn't given as much money to play with as he was used to.

Scott challenged Dennis. "Why don't you ask him when he gets here?"

Dennis laughed. "I don't want to upset that guy. I heard he's a lunatic on his movie sets."

Dennis was right and Scott secretly agreed. He believed that Jimmy Corn was the one wild card that could make or break the bar. He knew the rumors were true, but remained a loyal fan over the years and was willing to give him the benefit of the doubt.

While his films made lots of money for his producers, Jimmy quickly earned the reputation of being difficult. He was known to lock himself in trailers for days and threaten his cast with violence. First, certain studios refused to work with him. Then, the independent producers backed away. Once actors wanted nothing to do with him, Jimmy checked himself into a mental hospital and came out heavily medicated, but with a more balanced personality. The town believed in second chances, and he was getting one, but one with a short leash.

CHAPTER TWO
Strutter

Dennis worked on a crossword puzzle in his usual corner seat while Scott and Alison poured drinks. As a customer got up to leave, Scott reached under the bar and tossed a set of keys at him.

Others gathered around, reading the fliers about becoming movie extras. Scott couldn't help but notice. People were talking about it. The buzz was starting. Since he was such a big Jimmy Corn fan, he really campaigned for the movie to be filmed there. Combined with the future ownership of the bar, Scott felt like the fruits of all his labor were finally about to pay off.

Then the bar went silent as the jukebox changed songs.

It was at that moment the door opened and she walked in, just as a popular rock song blasted through the speakers. The regulars always had a habit of turning to look when someone walked in, and this was no exception.

Scott was pouring a beer when he first saw her. He was immediately smitten and lost all concentration on the drink he was fetching and let the glass overflow with beer. Her beauty hypnotized him.

Her long blonde hair cascaded down her back and her bright blue eyes lit up the room. Her slightly revealing red cocktail dress was perfection. Her entrance was like a model on the runway. It didn't matter who owned the bar on this day, yesterday, or next week. The goddess that just walked in owned the bar in that moment.

As she continued in what seemed to be slow motion, the bouncer, Troy, stopped her. He looked like a football linebacker who could also play basketball: muscular and very tall. He was supposed to card people at the door and somehow she slipped right by him, so he caught up and asked, "Can I see some ID, miss?" She seemed annoyed and rummaged through her purse, but Troy was just doing his job.

Beer continued to cascade from the glass, but Scott didn't care. Alison turned off the tap herself and punched Scott on the shoulder. "What are you doing?" she asked.

Alison followed Scott's eyes to the door and pointed. "Hey! Isn't that…"

Scott was still staring at her and replied, "She looks familiar."

Alison couldn't believe it. "Oh my god!"

Scott questioned himself. "No. It can't be. Can it?"

Alison announced, "Laura Summer!"

"What's she doing here?" Scott asked.

He seemed confused, but then it clicked and dollar signs filled the hearts in Scott's eyes. The customers were excited. The town was buzzing. Celebrities were already walking in. Scott's plan couldn't have gone any better.

He guessed, "She's probably friends with Shannon Green. We're becoming a Hollywood hotspot and we're in Pennsylvania! Ka-Ching!"

As Laura rolled her eyes and handed Troy her driver's license, Scott went into a panic. This was not the first impression he wanted her to have. Scott jumped over the bar and rushed to her side. He snatched the ID out of Troy's hand and gave it back to Laura without looking at it. "That won't be necessary."

Laura appreciated the star treatment and smiled at Scott. "Thank you."

Scott extended his hand out to her. She did the same, and while they shook hands, they stared into each other's eyes. Scott was in a trance. He couldn't believe what was happening. Finally, Laura broke the eye contact and looked around, waiting for Scott to say something. She seemed to get bored fast. He got the hint, his heart sighing in disappointment.

"I'm Scott. I'm the manager here. Actually, tomorrow I'll be on my way to being the new owner."

That appeared to make Laura feel more comfortable. She smiled again and said, "I'm Laura."

"I know. It's great to meet you. Come in and sit down."

Scott led her to a less crowded area of the bar near Dennis. As Laura sat down, Scott sprinted around the bar until he was directly across from her and bumped Alison out of the way. "Hey!" Alison yelled. She threw an ice cube at him and missed.

Scott announced, "Whatever you want, it's on the house."

Dennis overheard and chimed in. "My place still, Junior."

Scott didn't even look at Dennis. "Ignore that guy."

Laura made herself comfortable and placed her hands on the bar. "Water with lemon, please."

The request threw Scott off. He was expecting her to order a glass of wine or at least an imported beer. Laura was well known in the press as a heavy drinker. Scott replied, "Yes. On the way. No tap. Spring..."

"That's fine," Laura whispered as she twirled her hair impatiently.

Scott clumsily poured a glass of water as Alison nudged her way in front of her. "Don't mind him, Laura. He's star struck."

Laura smirked at Alison, then stared rudely at her face. Laura remarked, "Is this a funeral parlor? Did somebody die? What's with all the black makeup?"

Alison quickly turned the other way and pretended she didn't hear the comment. After a few moments, Alison disappeared from behind the bar and headed for the ladies' room. Laura watched her go and laughed while Scott placed the glass of water in front of her.

Laura scoffed, "What's her problem?"

Scott attempted to explain. "A couple of years ago, her fiancé..."

Laura interrupted, "Whatever. Nobody cares."

And just like that, Scott's brief infatuation with her was over. In mere seconds, she managed to insult his sister and cut off his explanation. This was normal behavior from his most rowdy, drunken customers, but she had to earn that privilege.

He held himself back from saying what he really wanted to say. All he could do was laugh.

Not at Laura, but himself, for actually finding her attractive in the first place.

He only got out, "So..."

Laura took a sip of her water.

He tried again. "So...what brings you to town?"

Laura was offended. She furrowed her eyebrows and swiftly answered, "I'm in the movie. Why else would I be here?"

"Oh really? You're in the movie too? I didn't know that. Who do you play?"

"I play Beth, the lead character. The bartender."

Scott laughed it off. "Shannon Green is playing the bartender."

"Wrong," Laura very matter-of-factly stated as she ran her hand through her hair. Scott could see she wasn't making it up.

"Since when?" he asked.

"Don't you read the trades?"

"The what?"

The tone of Laura's voice changed. "Shannon Green dropped out like a week ago. I'm the star!"

Scott was completely caught off guard. He looked over at Dennis who clearly heard the whole conversation. Dennis shrugged his shoulders. Before Laura walked in, Scott was on top of the world. Now he felt weak and vulnerable, like she was there to intentionally sabotage everything.

Laura seemed annoyed about having to explain herself as she looked around the bar for something to do. Grabbing the glass of water, she wiggled off her seat and danced her way to the jukebox.

Scott hurried over to Dennis and asked, "What's going on?"

"I talked to Victor today, but he didn't mention it."

"Can you call him please?"

"And say what?"

"You're friends with the man! You named your bar after him! He'll listen to you."

"Victor helped me buy this place twenty years ago. I'm not going to complain about anything. Be thankful he's shooting his movie here at all. What's it matter who the star is?"

Scott pointed at Laura as she scrolled through songs from the jukebox. "That girl is trouble. She will ruin the movie and she'll ruin this bar. My bar."

Dennis had nothing to say.

Up until now, Scott believed this movie was the best thing to ever happen to this town and the bar. Now he wasn't so sure. In his mind, Laura Summer could actually bring the value of the bar down, the bar he was about to buy in the morning!

Alison wiped tears from her eyes as she walked out of the bathroom. She passed by Laura at the jukebox and they exchanged dirty looks.

Alison stopped by Scott and Dennis on her way back. "You can wait on her. She's all yours."

Scott looked at a large black-and-white picture of a middle-aged man that was hanging on the wall. It was autographed with the name, Victor Cashman.

Dennis was right.

Scott quietly recalled a time when Victor Cashman was the most powerful producer in Hollywood. It took him over twenty years to achieve that lofty position. He started out with the usual schlocky B-movies and even survived unconfirmed rumors he produced adult films under a fake name.

His big break came when he produced the popular *Stuntman* superhero films with actor Garrison Banks, who portrayed the villain known as The Jackal. Each film in that series grossed nearly a billion dollars worldwide. Victor and Garrison continued to work together on low budget, but high grossing independent films that generated award nominations every year. Eventually, Garrison retired from acting and Victor was forced to collaborate with someone else.

Every film since then had been a box office failure, so he turned to reality television and found a hit with the ghost hunting series called *Spirit Chasers*. The success was short-lived though, as the show was abruptly canceled amidst rumors that they were staging hauntings for ratings. Many felt that *Pretty Ugly* was Victor's last chance to turn things around and get his career back on track. It was a comeback film for everyone involved; Victor, Jimmy and Laura.

Scott straightened the portrait of the smiling Victor as Laura danced her way back to the bar. Alison noticed that Laura was still obsessively staring at her. She gave Laura a few chances to stop, but Alison wasn't as good at ignoring obnoxious customers as Scott was.

Alison smacked the bar right in front of Laura. It got the attention of most of the patrons, especially Scott and Dennis. Laura was definitely startled and nearly fell off her seat.

Alison got right up in Laura's face. "What are you staring at? Do you have a problem with me?"

Scott stayed put, unsure of what to do. He just knew not to cross his sister when she was like that, but he was ready to pull her back if needed.

Calmly, Laura replied, "I'm watching you bartend because I am playing a bartender in this movie. I'm an actress. Remember?"

Alison purposely knocked over Laura's glass, spilling water all over her lap. Laura jumped back. "What the...?" Her look of shock quickly turned into disgust, and then to anger.

Alison laughed. "There's your first lesson. That's how you spill a drink on somebody you don't like."

Laura turned it on. "You stupid bitch!"

Scott quickly intervened and took his sister aside. "Alison, how about you call it a night?"

He had only once witnessed his sister act like this with a customer, and it did not end well. These two were headed for a bar brawl and Scott knew he had to prevent it.

Alison agreed. "Yeah. Good idea. I'm out of here."

Scott patted her on the back as she exchanged one more dirty look with Laura. Alison grabbed a few things and quickly hurried out the door.

Laura let out a sigh of relief as Scott placed a new glass of water in front of her. She shook her head. "Thank god. You should seriously fire her."

Scott had enough and needed to draw a line. While he was concerned about the damage she could do to the bar's image, he was also in protective brother mode. "Watch it. She's my sister and after tomorrow..."

Laura interrupted. "Can you take down the Shannon Green sign?"

Scott waited, then reluctantly reached up and tore down the sign. It dropped to the floor as Laura clapped her hands.

The sounds around him started to blend together. The music. Customers talking. Laura's clapping. Was this really happening? He wanted to wake up from this nightmare called Laura Summer. He kept looking at the door. Maybe Shannon Green would walk in and take the role back from Laura. Maybe Victor would come in and tell him Laura was fired.

As Laura took a sip of her water, Scott wanted so badly to smack it out of her hand and tell her to go home. The film shoot was supposed to take a month, but now it would seem like years. All he could think about was putting the movie behind him and sending her back to Los Angeles so he could focus on running his new bar. He didn't want to spend any more time with her than he had to. So much for looking forward to seeing a movie get shot. Not anymore.

As he thought about how to avoid her throughout the month, he reminded himself that she was still sitting across from him after just disrespecting his sister. He needed to put her in her place, but he had to be smart about it. He smiled as he thought of the easiest, most obvious way to take a shot at Laura and asked, "How's your father?"

"What?"

"Is he producing your movie?"

"What's that supposed to mean?"

"He got you on TV, on his shows. It's good to be the princess."

Laura went into full defense mode. "I had to audition for those parts!"

Scott countered, "The auditions were fake. You already had the part."

"I worked hard on those shows! I paid my dues!" Her jaw was tense, her teeth clenched. Scott knew he had to either call it quits or push her over the edge. It was an easy decision. He was actually starting to enjoy this.

He continued, "Bartending is a real job. No limo. No craft services. No agent. Just a day's work." Scott tossed a washcloth at her and added, "Why don't you come over to this side of the bar and do your research? Unless you're afraid you'll mess up your manicure?"

Laura reached out, grabbed Scott's arms and yanked him across the bar, over her seat and right onto the floor. Her glass of water shattered. She lifted Scott to his feet and said, "You've got nothing to say now, do you?"

Scott was still in shock that she pulled him to the other side of the bar. As he tried to process the situation, Laura landed a solid right hook on his chin. After he absorbed the punch, he remembered that she was no stranger to bar fights and that Tony Steel taught her a few Krav Maga moves when they started dating.

Dennis jumped out of his chair and stood between them as customers gathered.

He yelled, "Get out!"

Laura pointed to the door and glared at Scott while she shouted, "You heard the man!"

Dennis did a double take. He couldn't believe what he just heard. "Not him! You! Leave now!"

Laura swung her arm around and caused Dennis to flinch, but she only grabbed her purse. "Fine. This place is a dump anyway."

Laura threw her purse around her arm and took one last look around the bar.

"You'll never see me in here again! Not for a drink! Not for food! And definitely not to film a movie!"

She ended her tirade on Scott and gave him a look he would never forget as she bit down on her lip. He could feel the daggers in her eyes as she stared him down.

Laura took the first step to leave, but slipped on the water from the broken glass and hit her face on the edge of the bar. Scott reluctantly rushed to help her, but she pushed him away as she turned and ran out of the bar.

The customers erupted with applause as Scott returned to work. He was used to bar drama. It was part of the job. But this made him question his ability to run the bar. How did he let the situation spiral out of control so fast? He should have bit his tongue and let her be the spoiled movie star she was.

After a few minutes, Scott could feel his customers' eyes upon him. He pretended as though his jaw didn't hurt, but it did, and he tried not to touch it. He was embarrassed and wished it was closing time, but the night was young.

Scott noticed a pink cell phone lying on the floor and picked it up.

CHAPTER THREE
Silver Spoon

Victor Cashman was the embodiment of the slick, well-dressed Hollywood producer. He stood impatiently in the hotel hallway with a bottle of wine in one hand and pounded on a door with the other. He had been waiting for someone to answer for a while.

Finally, the door crept open. Victor looked both ways and then slithered in.

Sophia Summer closed the door behind him as Victor made himself comfortable on the bed. He looked around.

"Your daughter's not here, is she?"

"No, she went down to that bar to do some research on her part."

"The bar? She's by herself?"

"Stop it, Victor."

Sophia sat next to him on the bed.

"She's by herself?"

"She's doing good. She has a sponsor now and goes to meetings. AA is working wonders for her."

Victor was concerned. "I don't want any trouble. She had better behave herself."

"She'll be fine. She wants this to work. She needs this for her career."

"And if she goes over the edge? I heard about what happened last month in Bel Air."

The Bel Air incident somehow managed to stay out of the press, but rumors swirled in Hollywood that someone connected to the week long disaster was secretly writing a book about it.

"Yes, she had a little incident."

Victor sarcastically replied, "Little?"

"But she's back on track now. Who cares about what happened in Bel Air?"

"I will pull the plug. I swear. I can replace her with one phone call." Victor was right. He could easily replace her, but he was only making idle threats. He had too much riding on this project and already gambled by casting Laura. Hollywood was waiting for the production to implode and Victor was determined to prove the town wrong. He was prepared to fire Laura, but only as a last resort.

Sophia covered his mouth with her hand. "There won't be a problem. Okay?" With a sexy smile, she whispered, "Can we talk business over breakfast?"

Sophia snatched the bottle of wine out of Victor's hand while he unbuttoned his trousers. This was not the first night they ever spent together. Victor and Sophia's on and off relationship went back years. Everyone suspected they were seeing each other when Sophia's marriage to Seymour was on the rocks, but she always denied it.

Suddenly, the door to the room flew open and Laura burst in. She slammed the door behind her and dropped to her knees. Sophia pulled the covers over Victor before Laura could notice him.

"Mommy!"

Victor's leg hung off the edge of the bed. Sophia quickly yanked it out of view and joined him under the covers.

"Mom?"

Sophia barked, "Not right now, Laura! Go back to your room. We'll talk in the morning."

Throwing a temper tantrum, Laura punched the wall. Victor would normally laugh at Laura's behavior, but he was in the eye of the storm and preferred to stay quiet as long as possible.

"No, Mom! Now!"

Sophia angrily asked, "How did you get a key to my room?"

"The front desk knew who I was. I would have called you, but..." Laura struggled with her words, but got out, "I left my cell phone at the bar."

Sophia peeked her head out from under the covers. "Oh my god, Laura, have you been drinking?!"

"No!"

Laura climbed onto the bed, but quickly realized there was someone else there. She backed away and asked, "Who is that?"

Victor popped his head out for her to see and smiled.

"Victor?"

"Hi, Laura."

Laura kicked the bed.

"Mom! What are you doing?! God!"

"We're not having this conversation again, Laura. What happened to your face? Did you get into a fight?"

Victor didn't notice until Sophia pointed it out. He immediately went into panic mode and yelled, "The first shot is Monday and she has a black eye!"

Laura covered her face and ran out of the room. Victor and Sophia looked at each other, stunned. Sophia tried to kiss Victor, but he resisted.

"Really, Sophia? The first night? She can't even make it through one night?"

"We'll deal with her in the morning," Sophia answered as she disappeared under the covers.

Victor added, "She's going to need a lot of makeup to cover that up."

Sophia pulled Victor back under with her. He resisted at first, but quickly gave in.

The next morning, Victor and Sophia shared breakfast at a small table in the hotel's restaurant. They were both fully, and very nicely dressed. They didn't seem like they had just spent the night together. They were in full-on business mode.

Victor picked up right where he left off in the conversation about Laura. "She's here one night and already causing trouble. I'm having an anxiety attack here, Sophia, you told me..."

Sophia cut him off. "I can't watch her twenty-four hours a day." She took a breath and calmly added, "I have to go back to LA."

"No! You're her manager! Manage her!"

"I have other clients, deals to make, contracts to sign. You know this. I can't stay here with her. I'll talk to Laura. We'll make it work."

Sophia wasn't kidding. Her calendar was booked. She couldn't stay with Laura unless it was an absolute emergency.

"She needs a full-time manager. I have work to do. I can't produce this picture and babysit your little darling," he told her sternly.

"Then get somebody who will!"

"I already planned on it."

Victor tried his best to regain his composure and went back to eating his breakfast.

~ * ~

Upstairs in her room, Laura was still in her pajamas, asleep on the bed of her luxurious hotel suite. Her legs dangled off the side.

Knock. Knock. Knock.

Laura didn't move as the knocks continued. Then the knocks turned to pounding on the door.

She flinched, slowly sat up and looked around in a daze.

She struggled to string any words together but somehow managed to ask, "Who is it?"

She jumped up out of bed.

Sophia's voice echoed, "Laura, it's me. Open the door!"

"And Victor..."

Laura briefly froze, then ran over to the mirror and stared at her face.

"Oh no."

She grabbed some makeup off the dresser and attempted to smear it over the scratches, but it didn't work.

"Laura, we don't have all day," Victor said.

Laura looked at the clock, then back in the mirror and wiped the makeup off.

"Coming..."

Laura hurried to the door and opened it. Sophia immediately hugged her.

"Oh you poor thing! What happened?"

Victor slammed the door behind them. "I'm sorry, Laura. You're a wonderful girl, but this film is important to a lot of people. You just got out of rehab. You need more time to adjust. Go back home and get some rest."

Laura went on the defensive. "You're firing me?! I wasn't drinking!"

She turned to her mother and gave her an order. "Mom! Do something!"

Sophia just shrugged hopelessly as Victor headed for the door.

Laura pleaded, "No! Victor! Wait! Please!"

Victor paused, and without Laura seeing, winked at Sophia.

"Just give me a chance," Laura begged.

Victor turned and locked eyes with Laura. "If we work this out, you're going to have to follow some rules."

Laura agreed. "Whatever it takes."

"You're getting a manager," Victor added.

"But Mom is my manager."

Sophia chimed in, "I'm going back to LA, honey."

"Mommy!"

Sophia assured her, "We're going to get you help."

Laura was confused. "Help?"

Victor explained, "A bodyguard. Somebody to help you get through the day."

The room suddenly got quiet as Laura processed the idea. Victor snapped her out of her deep thought before announcing, "Now...I'm going over to the bar to do some damage control."

"No!" Laura chirped.

"What did you say to me?"

Laura lowered her voice. "Can we film the movie somewhere else? I don't like it there."

Victor did his best to put it to her nicely. "Laura, I believe in you. So I need you to believe in me. Let me produce and I'll let you be the star. Are we on the same page?"

As Victor opened the hotel room door, Laura begged, "Wait!"

"What?"

"If you're going to that bar, can you get my cell phone? I left it there last night. I'm sure someone found it. I need it so bad."

Victor gave Laura a sarcastic nod of approval. "For you, my dear, anything." He waved to Laura, then smiled at Sophia and left the room.

CHAPTER FOUR
You Love Me to Hate You

On the other side of town, Scott arrived at the bank to finalize the loan. He was dressed in a suit and carried a briefcase. He rarely wore a suit, but this was a special occasion. He cleaned up fairly well. You couldn't even tell he had been punched in the face the night before.

Once he was sitting at the desk across from the loan officer, he clenched a pen, ready to sign. And then he heard a word that seemed to echo throughout the room, "No." His heart pounded and a bead of sweat ran down his forehead. He couldn't remember how it was explained to him, as all the words that followed blended together. When the loan officer reached out to shake his hand, all he knew was he'd been denied.

Outside in his car, he just sat there in complete silence. He removed his tie and stared at himself through the rearview mirror. Getting hit by Laura Summer was nothing. Not getting the loan was a sucker punch to the gut. It knocked the wind out of him and he struggled to breathe. He wanted to throw up. He wanted to cry. He wanted to scream. But he held it all in and waited until he felt safe enough to drive. How was he going to break the news to Dennis?

At the bar, Scott walked in just as Dennis removed the last stool from atop the counter. Scott couldn't even look at him. He tossed his briefcase onto the bar and took a seat in the corner.

"Well?" Dennis asked. He waited for a response, but didn't get one.

Scott had a way of speaking to Dennis without words, something they developed over the years, whether it was nods, winks or smiles. Scott didn't have to tell him he had been turned down.

Dennis sat down next to him. "Did they tell you why?"

"Yeah, but I lost them when they started talking about numbers. I don't think I had enough collateral. I still owe too much on the house."

Dennis politely reminded him, "I have another buyer, Scott."

Scott asked, "Can you give me some time to come up with more money?"

Dennis countered, "Four weeks. That's the best I can do. That gives you until the movie crew leaves." For Scott, it wasn't enough time to come up with that kind of money. It wasn't something he could solve with a yard sale or by donating blood. This was big bucks.

But Scott assured Dennis with his usual confidence, "I'll figure something out. I always do." Scott believed that when one door closed, another one opened. And literally in that moment, the door to the bar swung open and the first customer of the day strolled in. It was Victor. He shouted, "Hey! Where is everybody?"

Scott and Dennis turned around to see Victor admiring his portrait on the wall. He winked at himself. Dennis climbed out of his seat to greet him.

"Victor!"

"Dennis!"

They shook hands, then gave each other a hug like long lost friends. Scott looked back and forth between Victor and his picture on the wall.

Dennis motioned to Scott. "This is my manager, the future owner, Scott."

Victor politely smiled. "Nice to meet you, Scott."

"Good to finally meet you, too. I love your movies, sir. *Deer in Headlights* was awesome."

They shook hands.

Scott wasn't used to meeting all these celebrities. He didn't know what to say, but did the best he could. "Thanks again for bringing the production here. It means a lot to me, and the whole community."

Victor looked around fondly. "This is my hometown. Besides, the place is named after me. How could I film a movie about a bar somewhere else?"

Victor pointed to a bar stool and reminisced, "My first beer was in that seat right there. I wasn't even twenty-one, and neither was Dennis."

Victor looked closer at the rickety wooden stool. It was covered with hand carved initials from over the years. He ran his fingers over the initials VC. He continued, "Back then, this place was called The Firehouse. Dennis and I used to get into all kinds of trouble here. Hey, remember the time..."

Dennis politely cut him off, "So how are things going?"

Victor laughed and switched gears into a more serious tone. "Actually, I heard you had a little trouble with Miss Summer last night."

Scott didn't waste any time cutting right to the chase. "Did she really replace Shannon Green?"

Victor sighed and informed him, "There's no guarantees in show business."

Dennis chimed in. "We're just happy to have you here. I hope last night's incident didn't affect your decision to film here."

Victor assured them, "No, not at all. But I was hoping you could do me a favor. I need some help."

"Sure. Anything," Dennis replied.

Victor announced, "I need a bodyguard. Someone to watch over Laura 24/7. I'm in a real bind here."

Scott and Dennis looked at each other.

Scott couldn't believe it. "Are you serious?"

"Absolutely. I need someone by her side at all times. Get her to the set and keep her from harming herself. She's a mess."

Scott shook his head and laughed. "My sympathy goes out to whoever takes that job. She's a piece of work."

Victor handed Scott a business card. "If you think of someone, give me a call. We are budgeted for this. It's very good pay."

"How much?" Scott instinctively asked.

"I don't know. Like a couple grand a week," Victor quickly replied.

Dennis glanced at Scott, "How much more cash do you need for the loan?"

"They told me I was short by about twenty grand," Scott answered.

Dennis turned to Victor. "Is that in the budget?"

"Depends. I need assurances, and you must be reliable."

"Scott's been my best employee for years. Never calls out. Never late."

Victor looked Scott right in the eye. "So you're interested?"

The whole thing happened so fast, Scott didn't have the chance to think about what he was signing up for, so he slowed things down a bit. "Hold on. Wait a second. What exactly do you need me to do?"

Victor explained, "Just make sure Laura's on time every day and keep her out of trouble. More like babysitting."

Financially, this was an easy decision for Scott, but personally, he was torn. He never wanted to be anywhere near Laura Summer again. His plan was to avoid her at all costs during the movie shoot. The previous night played over and over in his head. The way she treated his sister. The things she said about the bar. And that right hook. He grabbed his chin as if she'd just punched him again. Nope. There was no way he could spend the next four weeks babysitting a stuck-up, spoiled movie star like Laura Summer. He needed the money, but there had to be another way.

Scott shook his head. "I don't think I'm..."

Dennis didn't even let him finish the sentence. He grabbed Scott and pulled him aside. "What are you doing?"

Scott needed Dennis to keep him in check and remind him that this was an opportunity he wasn't going to get again. If he turned Victor down and couldn't raise the money himself, the bar would be sold to someone else. Laura Summer was the only thing standing between Scott and the bar. He knew what he had to do. Like Victor said, it was just babysitting. How hard could it be?

Scott extended his hand to Victor. "I'm your guy. I'll take the job."

"Done," Victor announced. "It's a deal." They shook hands.

Scott voiced an immediate concern. "Can you give me some kind of guarantee? She wasn't exactly friendly with me. I don't think she'll go for this."

Victor assured him, "She has no say. I do the hiring and the firing on my productions."

That was all Scott needed to hear.

~ * ~

On the other side of town in Sophia's hotel room, Laura watched her mother fill a suitcase with clothes.

"Mom, I don't understand why you can't stay."

"Honey, we've been through this over and over again."

Laura complained, "But I'm bored. I don't know anyone here."

"Not for long. Victor already hired a bodyguard for you."

Laura was surprised. "He did? Wow, that was fast!"

Sophia added, "He's sending him to pick you up at six for dinner. You'll be meeting Victor somewhere. Don't be late."

Under normal circumstances, Tony Steel served as her bodyguard. He shielded her from annoying fans and kept the paparazzi at arm's length. All the camera guys were afraid of him. At times, he was a bit overprotective. With Tony in Budapest, this was going to be Laura's first real bodyguard.

"Who is it? Do you know? Is he from LA? Is he hot?"

"I don't know anything about him."

"Please don't tell Tony," Laura begged.

"Why would I do that? You said he was out of the country anyway."

Laura frowned. "Tony would freak out if he found out about this." There was more to it than that. Laura knew that if Tony heard she had a bodyguard, he would be on the first plane into town. Tony was in Budapest and Laura wanted to keep it that way.

Laura sneakily asked her mother, "What should I wear?"

"Behave yourself."

"I'll try," Laura said, but she knew she hadn't been too convincing. Her mother knew her too well.

"And Victor said he located your cell phone and will send it with the bodyguard," Sophia added.

Laura danced around the room. "Yay! My phone!"

"And don't forget to pick your brother up from the airport tomorrow," Sophia reminded her.

"Ricky?" Laura asked.

Laura really didn't remember, because this was the first she was hearing about it.

"Oh, didn't I tell you? Jimmy has a small cameo for him in the film."

Laura stomped her feet like she did when she was on *My Little Robot*. It always worked then and she thought maybe it would work now. "Mom! This is my movie! Mine! And I'm trying to stay sober. He drinks like a fish. He'll ruin everything!"

"Be nice to your big brother. He's trying very hard, just like you."

There was always a rivalry between the Summer siblings, but both parents equally spoiled them. Laura always felt she was in competition with Ricky, but he didn't see it that way. He was more laid back and relaxed, while Laura was uptight about things like maintaining her public image and building her fan base.

Sophia closed her suitcase and planted a kiss on Laura's cheek.

"I'll call you when I land in LA. Be nice to your new bodyguard."

Laura pulled out her lipstick. "Oh, I will, mother. I will."

"You're so bad. You're just like me."

~ * ~

About an hour later, Scott strolled through the hotel lobby with Laura's pink cell phone and a single yellow rose. He took the elevator to the second floor and found room 217. He stood there for a moment, took a deep breath and knocked. Something told him this wasn't going to go well.

He waited patiently as he could hear someone running around the room. He still had his doubts as to whether he could go through with this. In his head, he repeatedly told himself, "Do it for the bar."

The door slowly opened to reveal Laura. Her hair and makeup looked as if she was attending a movie premiere and she was squeezed into a tiny, sexy black dress.

Her seductive smile lasted only a few seconds. She squinted her eyes once she recognized him.

"You!"

"Good," Scott proclaimed. "You remember me."

Laura angrily asked, "Why are you here?!"

He calmly informed her, "Victor sent me. I'm your bodyguard."

She slammed the door in his face.

Screams could be heard coming from behind the door. Then, she suddenly stopped and peeked out.

As if nothing was wrong, Laura softly asked, "Do you have my cell phone?"

"Right here." Scott held out the cell phone. Laura snatched it and slammed the door in his face again.

Scott assured her through the door, "Trust me, I'm only doing this for the money."

Screams could be heard again, followed by another round of silence. Then more screams. Scott could hear her talking to someone on the phone, but couldn't understand what she was saying. He put his ear to the door, but that didn't help.

Finally, the door opened back up. Laura gave Scott a death stare, so he showed her the yellow rose and offered, "I'm willing to forgive and forget if you are."

She snatched the rose from his hand, broke off the bud, tossed it to the floor and squashed it with her high heel. She handed the decapitated stem back to him.

Laura demanded, "Let's go meet Victor so you can tell him you're not taking the job. Okay?"

"Sorry, I really do need the money," Scott responded.

Laura inquired, "What's he paying you?"

"Obviously not enough," Scott sarcastically replied.

Laura countered, "I'll double it. Just walk away."

"He said you'd probably try something like that and promised to match your offer."

Laura let out another scream of frustration then slammed the door behind them and walked briskly ahead of Scott. He tried desperately to keep up with her.

At the restaurant, Scott and Victor sat on one side while Laura stared coldly at them from across the table. She rudely pointed at Scott.

"He's not even a bodyguard," she declared. "Why did you pick him? How am I supposed to feel safe? Did he tell you I kicked his ass last night? He's the one that needs a bodyguard. Not me."

Scott acted like he didn't know what she was talking about, but it didn't matter. Victor laid down the law right then and there. "Here's the rules: Scott will drive you. Everywhere you go, he goes. If you insist on going to a bar or a club, you leave when he says. When you are out in public, you listen to him. Scott will be staying in a room right next to yours. If you leave the hotel without him, you're fired."

Laura tried to comprehend what he just said, but she just couldn't seem to process it. "I don't get it. Why are you doing this to me?"

"Because that's the only way I can trust you on this movie. You either accept it or go home. Understand?"

There was a long silence at the table as her face contorted and twitched with defeat. Scott could feel her shooting laser beams out of her eyes at him, but knew she was surrendering. Victor had her backed into a corner.

Laura asked, "Does Tony know about all of this?"

Victor quickly answered, "No, but that's your decision. Personally, I wouldn't recommend it, and I really don't want that lunatic showing up here. I already have my hands full with you and Jimmy."

This was the first big movie Laura had the chance to star in since they had started dating and in the past, Tony Steel had made it a point to show up unannounced and wreak havoc on his prior girlfriends' movie sets. Rumors were that Victor paid a lot of money to make sure Tony got the starring role that required him to be in Budapest while Laura was filming.

Scott took the opportunity to inject himself into the conversation. "I used to be a huge Tony Steel fan. Still am. *Above Justice* and *Under Attack* were…"

Laura cut him off. "Nobody cares what you think."

Scott wanted to retaliate, but held back, as hard as it was. If this was a preview of the weeks to come, it was going to be a long, rough ride. He just had to convince himself it would be worth it in the end.

Victor rolled his eyes and reminded Laura, "You're going to be spending a lot of time with this guy, so get over it."

Victor stood up and looked back and forth between them. "Now, I'm going to leave the two of you alone. Try your best to get along and don't kill each other."

Once Victor left, Laura glanced around the restaurant as if Scott didn't exist. Seconds later, Victor returned and added one last thing. "Don't forget about rehearsal in the morning. Then you have that interview on *The Jackie and Bobby Show*. Don't be late for either one."

He pointed at Scott. "Make sure she's there."

Scott assured him, "No problem."

Laura was confused. "I still don't understand why I'm going on that show."

Victor reminded her, "Publicity. It's in your contract."

Scott asked, "Have you ever listened to Jackie and Bobby?"

Victor didn't seem too concerned. "No. Why?"

"She's going to need me to coach her on this. I listen to the show and there's a game they play with guests called Nail..."

Laura interrupted him again. "I'm not five. I can handle an interview."

Victor didn't seem too confident. "Are you sure about that, Laura?"

Laura just stared Victor down as her eyes grew wide. He backed off and returned his attention to Scott and said, "Call me if there's a problem."

Victor finally left them alone and a long, awkward silence began. Laura played with her phone as Scott tapped his fingers on the table. It annoyed her, so she glanced under the table and then kicked him fairly hard on the shin. She warned him, "You have no idea what you just got yourself into."

Laura stood up to leave and Scott followed with a slight limp that he shook off as he caught up to her.

CHAPTER FIVE
Reputation

Scott sat in a chair strategically placed outside Laura's door. He watched her doorknob slowly turn, followed by a slight creaking of the door.

Laura crept out into the hallway and gently closed the door behind her. She wore a disguise in the form of a long, brunette wig and dark, wraparound sunglasses. She hurried down the hall and didn't even notice Scott, who got up and chased after her.

Scott shouted, "Where do you think you're going?"

Laura froze. She turned around, lowered her sunglasses and glared at him.

"For a walk. Do you mind?"

"Sounds great. I could use some fresh air."

"No, that's okay. I'll be all right."

"You know I have to follow you," Scott politely reminded her.

Laura sighed. She knew the rules. "I want to go out."

Scott countered, "I thought you quit drinking."

She clarified, "I did. I just want to go dancing."

Scott knew exactly where to take her. "We can do that. I know a place."

"Then let's go," Laura exclaimed.

As Laura scurried down the hall, Scott shouted, "Nice outfit."

Laura gasped and kept going. He struggled to keep up as she walked even faster.

After a short drive in the car, they arrived at a local nightclub. The parking lot was full and you could hear music all the way outside. Laura kept herself a short distance from Scott as they walked inside. She sat in the first open seat, which conveniently didn't have an empty one next to it. Scott stood behind her and crossed his arms in what he believed to be a bodyguard stance.

Scott took a moment and thought about the easy money he was making. Maybe it wasn't such a bad gig after all. Piece of cake. He was getting comfortable with the job. Babysit Laura to own the bar. It was that simple. She was settling down a bit, too. Nothing he couldn't handle. He just had to keep his eyes on the prize.

As the DJ spun records from a booth overlooking the crowded dance floor, Scott suggested, "Let's move across the bar. There are two seats over there."

Laura shooed him away like a fly. "I'm fine right where I am. You can go over there if you like."

"I don't mind standing," Scott said.

"Would you please sit over there?" Laura insisted.

"No, thanks."

"I don't want people to think we're together. You know what I mean?" Laura explained.

Scott agreed. "That's fine. I get it. I'll step back a few feet." He wouldn't want people to think that either, concerned about being associated with a notorious party girl.

The bartender approached them. "What can I get you?"

"Club soda," Laura replied.

The bartender nodded and started making the drink.

Scott sarcastically added, "Nothing for me. Thanks."

Scott was willing to be cordial throughout this arrangement. She clearly wasn't interested in doing the same. He turned to Laura. "I have an idea. How about we completely start over?"

Scott held his hand out to her. "My name's Scott."

She smacked his hand away and fumed, "I warned you. Go away. Now. Or I will."

When Scott didn't budge, Laura grabbed her drink, growled at him, and then made her way to the dance floor. Scott watched as she bobbed and weaved to the music through the flashing lights and found her groove in the center of the dance floor.

It was Scott's job to watch her, so that's what he did as she danced the night away. He couldn't take his eyes off her for fear she would disappear on him. His mind had no choice but to wander as she danced. He thought about how she was worried people might think they were a couple. And of course, that got him to thinking about what it would be like if they were. It was every guy's dream to date a movie star. Scott had lots of friends who would trade places with him in a heartbeat. He thought Laura was attractive, but could never admit it now. This was strictly a business relationship.

Eventually, Laura was bumping and grinding with a random guy named Paul. The poor guy had no idea who he was flirting with as her disguise was definitely working. As the DJ changed songs, Laura stopped dancing and pulled Paul in for a kiss.

When Scott saw this, he realized something he never even thought about. Not only did he have to deal with Laura, he had to tolerate every guy she talked to. The arrangement just got worse.

When Laura and Paul were done making out, she led him by the hand over to Scott.

"This is Paul. He's coming back to the hotel with me."

Scott gave Paul a courtesy smile and pulled her aside where he couldn't hear. "Laura, what are you doing? Does this guy even know who you are?"

"No. I don't think so."

Scott asked, "Don't you think maybe you should tell him?"

"Maybe I'd rather keep him in the dark," Laura replied.

Scott tried to talk some sense into her the only way he could. "What about Tony Steel?"

Laura quickly responded, "What about him?"

Scott realized he overstepped his bounds and backtracked, "Never mind."

"Yeah, that's right. It's none of your business," Laura said as she returned to Paul's side. For the first time, he agreed with Laura. Her love life was none of his concern. Besides, Scott heard many reports over the years that Laura and Tony both saw other people and that their relationship was just for show. Still, Tony was known to angrily dispute those rumors.

Scott tossed some cash on the bar and pulled out the car keys. He couldn't wait for the night to be over.

In the car, Scott played the role of chauffeur as Laura and Paul continued their make-out session in the back seat. Scott occasionally glanced at them in the rearview mirror, but each time made him more and more uncomfortable.

When they reached the hotel, Laura led Paul by the hand with Scott only a few steps behind until they reached their hotel rooms. Scott stood in front of his door while Laura and Paul stood in front of hers. Laura dug through her purse until she found her key.

Scott waved to Laura, but she ignored him. Paul kissed the side of her face as she opened the door and pulled him in with her. Laura kicked the door shut.

Scott stood there for a moment and listened to the giggles and kinky screams coming through her door. He thought about what he got himself into. Was this going to happen every night? He kept repeating in his head, "Do it for the bar. Do it for the bar." He laughed it off and headed to his room. It took longer than expected to get Laura out of his head and fall asleep, but he did.

The next morning, Scott waited outside Laura's room as he kept looking at his watch. She was cutting it too close. He had to wake her up. He wasn't looking forward to seeing this Paul guy again, but he had no choice and pounded on Laura's door until she answered.

She opened the door, but only enough to talk.

Laura could barely say, "What?"

Scott politely reminded her, "You're going to be late for rehearsal."

He still couldn't see Laura, but she replied, "I'm getting ready. Give me five more minutes." There was something about her tone. She wasn't talking down to him. It was a gentle, much kinder voice. Almost too nice.

Scott could only assume that something was wrong and asked, "Are you okay?"

Laura peeked her head out just enough for Scott to see one of her eyes. She nodded her head "no" and slowly closed the door. As a bartender, Scott was used to listening to other people's problems, so much so that he often considered himself a part-time therapist. It was a natural reaction for him to be concerned, even for those he wasn't fond of. He wanted to try to talk to her through the door, but decided to wait.

A short time later they were in the car and on their way. Laura's hair was pulled back in a ponytail and she barely wore any makeup.

Scott asked, "Do you want to talk?"

Laura calmly replied, "No."

There was a long silence.

Scott continued anyway and asked, "Did that guy do something to you?"

It was obvious she wanted to talk to anyone but Scott, but he had the advantage of being the only one who could listen to her in that moment. Just as he expected, she opened up and said, "He figured out who I was. I think he knew the whole time."

Scott wasn't surprised. "You can only hide it for so long."

Laura continued, "And then he asked me to do the robot dance and I lost it. I beat the crap out of him. I think I broke his nose."

Scott laughed, and then stopped himself. "All because he asked you to do the robot dance?"

Laura challenged, "Want to try me?"

Scott had last seen those fireballs in her eyes right before she clocked him the night they met. "No, thanks."

Scott laughed again, and a few seconds later, so did Laura. There was even a hint of a smile as she looked over at him.

Scott recalled reading about all the requests Laura had received over the years to perform the robot dance for commercials, but she always declined. No matter how much money they offered, she wasn't interested. Not that she needed the money. She even passed on a *My Little Robot* reunion with the original cast because the contract required her to perform the dance. The backlash from the fans was brutal and Scott quietly wondered why she despised the robot dance so much.

Before falling asleep that night, Scott went online and searched for episodes of *My Little Robot*. He remembered watching it when he was a kid, but seeing it now was a completely different experience. As he played clips of a young Laura Summer doing the robot dance, he found it cute and nostalgic and didn't understand why she had such a hatred for it. He made it a personal challenge to get her to perform the dance, even if it was just for him.

~ * ~

Over on the *Pretty Ugly* movie set, Victor watched Jimmy Corn from a distance. Jimmy was wild-eyed and fidgety as he held a clipboard and sipped from a cup of coffee. Victor could sense he was strung out and didn't want to get too close. Jimmy was already living up to his powder keg reputation.

Laura's co-star, Matt London, sat nearby and paged through a copy of the script. In typical Hollywood fashion, Matt was cast as the "ugly" guy, even though he was quite handsome and muscular. He wasn't Victor's first choice to play opposite Laura. He technically never acted before, but was a household name because his reality prank television show, *Jerk*, was a ratings smash on Sunday nights.

A male assistant placed a cup of coffee in front of Matt and another cup in front of the empty seat next to him. This was clearly Laura's seat. She wasn't late yet, but she was cutting it close.

Victor was more worried about Jimmy at the moment. He started to walk toward him, and then stopped. He moved a few steps closer. Victor was normally confident about everything, but for some reason, he was nervous that day. He waited for the right moment, then quickly approached him and blurted out, "The title has to go, Jimmy."

Jimmy looked up at Victor as if in slow motion. His eyes went wide and psychotic. Victor knew there was no such thing as good timing with Jimmy. He saw an outburst coming, but preferred to get it over with.

Jimmy violently stood up and threw his cup of coffee as hard as he could at the assistant who let out a soft scream before running off.

"Damn it, Victor! You promised me there wouldn't be any more changes!"

Victor stood his ground and insisted, "*Pretty Ugly* is not a good title for a chick flick."

The clipboard was next. Jimmy threw it across the set. Script pages went flying. "Stop calling it a chick flick! I'm not changing the title."

Victor grunted to himself, while the assistant picked up the clipboard and tried to hand it to Jimmy, but he kicked it out of his hand. Nobody was willing to roll the dice and make eye contact with him. Instead, everyone quietly waited for the next bomb to go off.

Jimmy broke the silence and screamed, "What do they want to call it?"

Victor's response seemed prepared. "Song titles are catchy. Like the movies *When a Man Loves a Woman* or *Can't Buy Me Love*. How about a Beatles song, Jimmy? How do you feel about calling the film *Love Me Do*?"

Jimmy repeated back, "*Love Me Do*?" He said it again. And again. He got angrier and angrier each time he said it.

Victor put his hands together in agreement and tried to calm the situation. "I like the way you said that Jimmy. Sounds like a hit already!"

"You want a Beatles song? I'll give you your damn Beatles song. How about *Helter Skelter*? You want that one? I think I like the sound of that."

The assistant raised his hand. Jimmy and Victor looked over at him as he informed them, "*Helter Skelter* was already made into a TV movie about Charles Manson."

Jimmy boiled over. "You think I didn't know that?"

Jimmy lunged at the assistant, but Victor held him back. As the assistant cowered on the floor, Jimmy pushed Victor out of the way and climbed onto the table.

Even jokester Matt backed away in his chair. This wasn't a prank. It was the real deal.

Jimmy asked, "What do you think Matt? Should we name our movie after a song?"

Matt didn't know what to say, so he nervously responded, "I'm just an actor. What do I know?"

Jimmy continued, "How about *Light My Fire*? Anyone like that song?"

Jimmy picked up an unattended script and held it in the air. He pulled a lighter out of his pocket and lit the script on fire.

Matt and the assistant backed away from the table. Victor wasn't fazed. He was used to this kind of behavior from him.

Just as the script went up in flames, the door opened and Laura and Scott entered the room. They froze near the door as Jimmy tossed the flaming script at Laura. It landed on the floor and Scott stomped out the small fire.

Laura could only say, "Oh my god! What's going on?"

Victor informed her, "Jimmy is motivated, I think. Brilliant man. Love ya, Jimmy."

Jimmy banged his fists on the table as Laura tiptoed around him and stood next to Matt. They never met before so she introduced herself.

"Hi. I'm Laura Summer."

"Matt London."

They didn't even look at each other or shake hands. Neither one could take their eyes off of Jimmy.

As the assistant handed Laura a new copy of the script, Jimmy jumped off the table and pointed at Laura and Matt. "Now, are you guys ready to make a movie?!"

Scott looked over at Victor who smiled nervously at him and gave a thumbs-up.

CHAPTER SIX
Radioactive

Т*he Jackie and Bobby Show* was one of the biggest morning radio programs on the East Coast. It was a double-edged sword for stars though. Their audience was so large, celebrities had no choice but to do the show when asked. If a star declined an interview, Jackie and Bobby would publicly ridicule and shame them on the air.

They were two very different personalities. Jackie was more of a frat-boy DJ, while Bobby was the voice of reason, making them a deadly combination of potty humor and intelligence. You never knew what to expect from them.

Laura sauntered into the radio show and sat in front of a microphone and put on headphones while Jackie and Bobby checked her out. Laura looked good and gave off a vibe that she knew it. Scott waited outside the room but could see into the studio through a glass window and hear the show over the building's speakers.

When they came back from commercial, Jackie laughed into the microphone as if he just heard a joke and then announced, "Welcome back. Today we have a very special surprise guest. Please welcome to the show for the first time, our favorite little robot movie star, Miss Laura Summer!"

The sound of applause filled the airwaves.

Laura smiled and leaned into the microphone. "Hi, Jackie. Hi, Bobby. Thanks for having me."

Bobby flipped through a tabloid magazine.

Jackie continued, "So, Laura, you're in town filming *Pretty Ugly*, the new Jimmy Corn movie. Can you tell our listeners a little bit about it?"

"Well, I like to describe it as a cross between *Pretty Woman* and *Coyote Ugly*."

Jackie asked, "A hooker at a bar? Is that what it's about?"

Laura quickly corrected him. "No, actually, it's a romantic comedy about a pretty bartender that falls for an ugly customer."

"Ahhh. I get it. *Pretty Ugly*."

Bobby jumped into the conversation. "Do you play the customer or the bartender?"

They all laughed, except Laura.

Jackie tried to help her out. "No, Bobby was just kidding. I'm sure you play the hot bartender. Who plays your love interest? The customer you fall in love with?"

"Matt London," Laura answered.

"Really? I didn't know he was in it. We've got to get him on the show. Does Matt get to make out with you in the movie?"

Laura smiled. "Maybe."

"What a lucky guy. We should get in the movie business," Jackie commented.

Bobby chimed back in and asked, "So Laura, we have to ask, what's going on with this sex tape?"

Laura appeared completely caught off guard. "Sex tape? I don't know anything about a sex tape."

Immediately concerned, Scott moved closer to the window. He could see the fear in Laura's eyes. He was worried something like this would happen.

Jackie pulled up a video clip on the computer screen in front of him and said, "Somebody e-mailed us a clip of it this morning."

Bobby added, "It's only a ten-second clip though."

Jackie confirmed, "It's definitely you."

Bobby pointed to something on the screen. "We think that's Tony Steel."

Laura was at a loss for words. "I really don't know what you're talking about."

As Laura squirmed in her chair, Scott felt uncomfortable for her. He wanted to stop the interview, but they were too far along. He wanted to coach her on what to say, but knew she would never listen to his advice anyway.

Jackie asked, "You want to see it?"

"No!" Laura yelled.

Audio from the sex tape played over the air. It was clearly Laura's voice, and she knew it.

Bobby tried to explain, "It's only a matter of time before the whole thing shows up on the internet. Someone's threatening to release it."

Laura was trembling, but nicely asked, "Can we talk about something else please?"

Scott banged his fist on the glass and they all looked, including Laura. Scott moved his hand across his neck and mouthed the word, "Cut." He learned something from his first day on a movie set.

It worked. Jackie shifted gears. "You want to play a game?"

Laura smiled at Scott through the glass. She acknowledged him and they shared a moment. It was brief, but it was enough to make Scott feel like he was doing something right, like he had done his job and protected her, and Laura had recognized that and appreciated it.

Laura quickly answered, "Sure."

Bobby recommended, "How about Guess the Number?"

Jackie shouted, "Yeah!"

Scott was still glowing from Laura's acknowledgment so it took a moment for him to realize what they were up to. He waved his hands, but Laura didn't notice.

Bobby jumped right into the game. "I'm going to risk my life here and say a hundred."

Jackie laughed. "Wow! I'm not going there. I'll have to say twenty."

Laura seemed confused. "What are you guessing?"

Scott went into a panic and banged on the glass again, but it was too late. Nobody paid him any attention this time.

Jackie nonchalantly told her, "How many dudes you've been with?"

Laura gasped and pointed at Bobby. "Did he say a hundred?"

The studio erupted with more canned laughter. Laura removed her headphones and threw them at Bobby.

Jackie filled in his listeners, "Wow! She's pissed. She just threw her headphones at Bobby."

If Scott were in there, he would have thrown something at them as well. He pressed his middle finger up against the glass. Bobby saw it and returned the gesture.

Laura glared at Jackie and lunged at him. A struggle could be heard over the air. Scott hurried into the studio and pulled her away from Jackie, as Bobby jumped between them. Laura stormed out with Scott right behind her.

Jackie's voice echoed through the hallway as he informed the listeners, "We're okay folks. She's gone now."

Bobby seemed excited. "That's the first time we've ever been attacked on the air. I don't think she was too happy with us. Do you think she'll be back?"

Jackie retorted, "She's not welcome back."

While Jackie and Bobby laughed over the speakers, Laura stopped in the lobby and waited for Scott to catch up. He attempted to put his hand on her shoulder, but she pushed him away.

Laura could barely speak. "I want to leave right now."

Scott couldn't agree more. In fact, he wished they could just disappear. As Scott reached into his pocket for the car keys, Laura smacked him across the face.

He was stunned at first, and then asked, "What was that for?"

Laura explained, "You just stood there and let them make fun of me like that."

Scott tried to argue, "But..."

Laura continued, "You're my bodyguard. You're supposed to protect me. From everything."

"But..."

She added, "I was just starting to think that maybe, just maybe, this might work out, but I'm not impressed. Not at all."

Scott countered, "What was I supposed to do?"

Laura looked at her watch. "It doesn't matter now. It's over. We have to pick up my brother from the airport. We're late. Let's go." And just like that, Laura shrugged the radio show disaster off. Scott wondered if that was how she always dealt with things.

This was the first Scott was hearing about Ricky's arrival. "Ricky Summer? What's he doing here?"

Scott only signed up to watch Laura. Nobody said anything about babysitting two Summers for the price of one. If he was responsible for both, this was going to cost Victor more money.

Laura seemed annoyed just at the mention of Ricky's name. "Victor promised him a small part in my movie. He's been a pain in my ass my whole life. I hope he missed his flight."

Scott followed Laura out of the lobby and into the parking lot.

At the airport, Laura sported her large sunglasses and brunette wig while Scott scanned the crowd for Ricky. "I haven't seen him in any movies recently, so I might not recognize him."

"Trust me. He looks exactly the same," Laura said.

They waited a little longer, and then Scott pointed at something in the distance. "I think I see him, but it doesn't look good."

Laura asked, "Where?"

"Coming right toward us."

Laura watched as two airport security guards escorted a man across the terminal. It was Ricky Summer.

Laura seemed disgusted. "What is wrong with him? I hate him!"

Scott couldn't wait to hear the story behind it. "This ought to be good."

A closer look at Ricky revealed bloodshot eyes, ripped jeans and a t-shirt that proclaimed, "I Know Ricky Summer."

His hands were cuffed behind his back and the security guards each held him by an arm. The guards smiled like teenage fans when they saw Laura.

"I hope you're taking him to jail," Laura told them.

"They're letting me go," Ricky bragged. "But I need you to do one thing."

Without hearing what it was, Laura simply answered, "No."

Ricky explained, "If you pose for a picture with these nice gentlemen, we can be on our way."

One of the guards pulled a cell phone from his pocket as the other removed the cuffs. Scott could tell that Laura was reluctant. She hesitated and seemed nervous. Scott just figured it was out of fear they would ask her to do the robot dance. Part of him was hoping they asked her to do the robot dance, just to see her reaction in person, but they didn't.

Laura filled her end of the bargain and let the guards take as many pictures as they wanted. She even smiled for some of them.

In the car, Ricky bounced around in the back seat. He flicked Laura's ear and asked, "Are you going to introduce me to your friend?"

Laura grabbed her ear, then turned and wound up to punch him, but held back. "He's not my friend. He calls himself a bodyguard. I don't even remember his name."

Scott waved at Ricky through the rearview mirror. "Hi. I'm Scott."

Ricky laughed. "I know who you are. You having fun yet? My sister's crazy, isn't she?"

Laura asked, "Were you drinking on the plane?"

"Hell, yeah. The stewardess recognized me, so she kept hooking me up."

Laura wondered, "How did you get in trouble this time?"

Ricky proudly announced, "The Mile High Club."

Scott was confused. He was a member of The Mile High Club too. He knew it happened on lots of flights. "They arrested you for that?"

Ricky added, "We never made it to the bathroom. I didn't think anyone was watching."

Laura rolled her eyes while Scott tried not to laugh. It was a typical Ricky Summer story that was probably going to end up in the tabloids.

They arrived at Victor's Bar and Grill to find it completely packed. Laura was still wearing her brunette wig and so far was not recognized, but several young female fans immediately surrounded Ricky. Scott sensed that Laura was jealous by the way she ignored Ricky's fans.

Dennis passed by Scott and said, "Tomorrow's the big day. How's everything going?"

Scott nodded toward Laura. "She's keeping me busy. I just stopped by to check on the place."

"I'm sorry I let Victor have you. I'm going crazy around here without a manager," Dennis informed him.

"Tomorrow, we close to the public, so things should get easier," Scott assured him.

Dennis kept moving as Scott and Laura headed to the corner of the bar. Alison was busy making drinks, so Scott just watched Ricky pose for pictures with women. It even looked like he got some phone numbers too.

Ricky rejoined them just as Alison reached their end of the bar. Alison and Laura's eyes locked. They remembered each other all too well and their exchange of dirty looks picked up right where they left off.

Laura whined, "Can we go somewhere else? It's bad enough I have to film here."

Alison approached Ricky as he pulled out a wad of cash and a credit card. Ricky argued, "No, we're staying. Everything's on me." Ricky waved his arm and yelled, "In fact, get the whole bar a round."

Customers cheered him on while Laura pinched him and grabbed him by the arm. Ricky squirmed and shouted, "Let go! We're not little kids anymore!"

Laura insisted, "We're leaving!"

"No! I'm celebrating! I just found out I got a part in the new TV show about the classic horror movie stars. It's called *Dude of 1,000 Faces*. I'm playing young Lon Chaney."

Laura laughed. "I don't even know who that is."

Ricky argued, "Yes you do."

Scott was quick to fill her in. "*Hunchback of Notre Dame. Phantom of the Opera.*"

Laura glared at Scott while Alison placed "free drink" chips in front of the other customers.

When Alison reached the register, she listened to Laura and watched her out of the corner of her eye.

Laura complained, "I still don't understand why you're here, Ricky. This is my movie. Mine. Go back home. Please?"

Alison leaned over to Laura. "That's the way you treat your own brother? No wonder you have no friends or fans anymore."

Laura started to reach for Alison but Ricky batted her hand down. Scott admired the way Ricky handled that. Simple and effective. He saw a brother and sister relationship similar to his and Alison's. Ricky reminded Laura, "She's just telling it how it is. I like that."

Still, Alison and Laura continued to stare each other down.

Alison softly whispered to Ricky, "By the way, all my friends had a crush on you because of the Venice Beach show, including me."

Laura was taken aback and remarked to Scott, "So your sister's a Goth bitch and a slut! Should've known."

Scott had a feeling of deja vu. His natural reaction was to stick up for his sister, but he and Laura had made a lot of progress in tolerating each other and he didn't want to ruin it. He tried to think of a clever thing to say to diffuse things, but was distracted as Ricky put his arm around him.

"Wait a minute. You didn't tell me that was your sister." Ricky said it loud enough for everyone to hear, as he eyed up Alison.

Laura seemed uncomfortable with Ricky's new potential love interest. She pushed him out of her way and got right in Scott's face. "I want to leave. Now! Tomorrow's the first day of shooting. Besides, if I'm in this place one more minute, I'm going to throw up. And it smells."

Scott didn't really have a choice. He still had to honor her wishes. He waved goodbye to Alison as Laura tugged on Ricky's shirt, but he resisted.

He informed her, "You can leave, sis, but I just got into town. I'm staying here."

Laura asked, "How are you going to get to the hotel? You didn't even check in yet."

Ricky didn't show any concern. "I don't worry about that kind of stuff. I'll find a way. I always do."

Alison added with a condescending tone, "I'll give him a ride. Go get your beauty sleep. You need it."

Laura put up her fists and was ready to fight Alison right then and there, but Ricky kept pushing her away. Scott made a mental note of how quickly Laura's buttons could be pushed, and how easily Ricky was able to handle her. Eventually, Laura followed Scott out of the bar but looked back several times at Alison.

Scott took Laura back to the hotel without incident. They both needed a good night's sleep before the first official day of filming.

CHAPTER SEVEN
Tears are Falling

Security guards blocked off a row of trailers in the bar's parking lot. Random onlookers watched from afar as a camera, sound gear and other movie equipment were set up near the entrance to Victor's Bar and Grill. Crew members stood around with nothing left to do.

Victor watched as Jimmy Corn angrily paced the set with a machete in his hand. Crew members noticed, but pretended not to. Matt London sat in a chair and watched Jimmy's every move.

Victor approached Jimmy from behind and caught him off guard. "Jimmy! What do you think you're doing?!"

"I'm making a movie," Jimmy replied.

Victor cut right to the chase. "What's going on with the machete?!"

Jimmy screamed, "Fear me!" Then he shouted louder for the whole set to hear, "Everyone should fear me!"

Victor calmly told him, "Well, you're off to a great start because Laura Summer is afraid to come out of her trailer!"

Jimmy's head looked like it was about to burst into flames. "Does she want me to come in there and drag her out? Because I will. By her hair."

Victor was already growing tired of the games. "Jimmy, we talked about this. Many times. Remember? No threats. No weapons. Either give me the machete or go back in your trailer and put it away so we can start the movie. Okay? Laura's bodyguard is trying to get her to come out, but you're going to have to put that down first."

Jimmy had nothing more to say and turned and walked toward his trailer. He swung the machete wildly in the air the entire way and mumbled obscenities. Victor watched the freak show as he moved across the set. Matt let out a sigh of relief as Victor smiled and waved at the behind the scenes cameraman who got the whole thing on tape.

Matt hurried to Victor for some kind of explanation of what had just happened. Victor saw him coming and simply stated, "We're almost ready to start!" Victor could see that Matt was upset and ready to complain, but avoided him by heading in the opposite direction.

~ * ~

Back in her trailer, Laura sobbed as someone knocked on the door. She yelled, "Go away!" She looked in the mirror and tried to wipe the tears from her eyes. She didn't want to let anyone see her crying like that. Her mother was the only one she let see her cry. Not her father. Not her brother. Not Tony. Nobody, and she intended to keep it that way.

She heard Scott call out, "Laura, it's me. Let me in." As she unlocked the door, Scott pushed his way through and stood in front of her. "Is this how movie sets normally operate?"

Laura answered, "No. He's nuts. I can't work under these conditions. I'm scared." She shielded her swollen eyes from him the best she could.

"I think Victor calmed Jimmy down," Scott assured her.

Laura still didn't feel safe and muttered, "For now. Have you seen my brother?"

"He's inside the bar helping my sister with the catering people."

Laura had a desperate look in her eye. "I need you to help me then."

Scott sat down next to her on the sofa and said, "Victor told me you won't come out."

Laura didn't feel she needed to provide an explanation. "Have you looked around? There's a maniac out there waving a knife. Not only is he the director, but somehow I need to tell him that I'm not doing the scene today."

Scott looked confused and scratched his head. "What was that last part you said?"

Laura repeated, "I'm not doing the scene."

Scott argued, "I think that's a very, very bad idea. You need to go out there and do what they're paying you to do."

"No! And I want you to tell him for me," she demanded. Scott just gave her a blank stare. Laura was testing him. Up until now, she only barked simple, generic orders at him. She knew she was going beyond the expectations of his job, but it was worth a shot.

"Me?! Tell him that? Are you crazy? He'll slit my throat with that thing. Why can't you just do the scene?"

"I'm not ready," Laura exclaimed.

Scott offered, "You want me to help you go over your lines?"

"That won't help."

"Why not?"

She explained, "They want to shoot the last scene of the movie first. I'm not ready for that scene. I can't do it."

"I still don't understand. What's the problem?"

"It's a very emotional scene. I have to cry!"

Scott laughed. "It looks like you were just crying! Go out there and shoot the scene! You're ready!"

"No, I'm not ready! And I wasn't crying either! God!"

All Scott got out was, "But..." before Laura cut him off. How dare he accuse her of crying?

"You don't know what it's like when there's a camera and all these people standing around watching you. It's too much pressure. I can't do it." When Laura first read the script on the airplane, she was so engrossed in the story, she didn't even realize her character had a crying scene at the end.

"They're all waiting for you. Are you coming out or not?"

Laura wouldn't back down. "Tell them this is my only request. I want to shoot this scene on the last day. That's it. I won't ask for anything else. Can you just do this one thing for me?"

"I don't know. This is something you should really tell them yourself."

Laura begged, "Please? For me? Jimmy's holding a meat cleaver!"

Scott looked into Laura's eyes. She was being sincere. She was legitimately scared, and actually had a right to be. He gave her a reassuring smile and then said, "I'll take care of it."

Laura didn't normally give hugs, but she felt an irresistible urge to hug Scott. As she wrapped her arms around him, she felt his heart rate spike. The feeling was mutual as Laura got all warm and fuzzy inside. In that moment, Laura trusted him and whispered, "Thank you."

Once Laura released Scott from her long, unexpected hug, he quickly exited the trailer. As Laura watched through the window, she couldn't explain it, but was mad at herself for not taking the opportunity to kiss Scott. Nothing passionate, but a quick peck on the lips or cheek to show her appreciation. Or something deeper?

~ * ~

Outside, Jimmy and Victor waited near the crew. There was no weapon in sight. They saw Scott coming, but without Laura. Jimmy waved his arms in the air, ready to flip out at a moment's notice.

As Scott approached them, he wondered if he was doing the right thing. After all, he was just Laura's bodyguard. Who was he to start making demands for her? With each step, he felt duped by her flirtatious hug. She got what she wanted. He thought about turning around and making her do her own dirty work, but it was too late. All eyes were on Scott for an explanation.

Victor asked, "Where is she?"

"She's not ready," Scott replied.

Victor wasn't having it. "Too bad. Everyone else is."

Matt joined them as Jimmy got right up in Victor's face. Jimmy screamed, "It's the first day! You're going to let her pull a stunt like this? If you don't take care of it, I will."

Scott pleaded her case. "Hold on! She just wants to shoot this scene last. She says it's the last scene of the movie, and that's the way she wants to film it."

Jimmy didn't seem too happy with what he heard. "Victor, who is this kid again?"

Victor informally introduced him. "This is Laura's bodyguard, Scott."

"Oh, okay. I thought Tony Steel was her bodyguard."

Scott tried to say something, but Jimmy didn't let him get one word out and screamed, "I hate Tony Steel!"

Jimmy moved his attention from Victor and took an aggressive stance toward Scott. "The way she wants to film it, huh? I'm the director! I film it the way I want to film it!"

As fast as he could, Scott explained, "She said she won't ask for anything else, just this one request." Scott closed his eyes, afraid of what would follow. He didn't know if Jimmy was going to punch him or try to slice him in half.

Indeed, Jimmy's hands reached out to strangle Scott, but Victor stepped between them and sided with Scott. "How bout it Jimmy? Can we shoot this scene last? It actually does make a little bit of sense."

Jimmy looked away and went into deep thought for a while. Everyone was on edge. Jimmy stared at all the camera gear and then finally answered, "I guess I can spend the day with the crew shooting B-rolls."

Sighs of relief filled the air, but not from Matt. He was ready to blow a gasket. "You're going to let her get away with this?"

Matt kicked his chair, pushed the production assistant out of his way and stormed off the set. He furiously ran to Laura's trailer and picked up a handful of rocks along the way. He threw one rock after another at her trailer.

Victor motioned for Scott to hang back. This was between Laura and Matt and it was best to let them work it out.

Seconds later, the trailer door slightly opened and Laura carefully peeked out as she clenched her cell phone. "Oh my god! Matt? What are you doing?"

"You know what, Laura? I worked my ass off to be ready for this scene. Who do you think you are?"

Laura fired back. "Don't go there, Matt! I'm the star of this movie and you know it."

"The star? You were a star, like ten years ago! You're probably the one who leaked your own sex tape!"

"What did you just say to me?"

Matt showed no fear of her. "You heard me."

Laura fumbled her words to retaliate. "Well, you're nothing but a stupid reality TV show contestant! You're not even an actor, Matt. You do pranks and stunts. You are a nobody!"

Those words bounced right off of Matt. "You know what, Laura? Everyone else in this movie believes in it and we're all working hard, including myself, so why don't you go back to your daddy's mansion in Beverly Hills so we can find an actress who actually cares!"

Laura opened her mouth, but nothing came out. No response. She was out of ammunition.

Matt turned and walked away as Scott sat in a lawn chair to give everyone some space, including Laura. He caught her watching him through the window a few times. She seemed to be calming down. After a while, she smiled at him and waved. He wasn't sure, but it even looked like she blew him a kiss.

~ * ~

When the dust settled, Jimmy sat on the steps of his trailer while Victor hovered over him and said, "I have to know, Jimmy. I have to know if you're okay. You can't scare the cast and crew like that again. Why would you do something like that on the first day?"

Jimmy had his reasons. "Last night, I was reading a message board on the internet and they're ripping me to shreds for making this film."

Victor assured him, "They'll still go see it."

"They don't want a love story from me," Jimmy argued. "They want guns. They want blood."

Victor did his best to comfort him. "On the next one, Jimmy. On the next one."

Jimmy announced, "I rewrote the script."

Waving a machete around was one thing. Rewriting the script? Now Victor was legitimately concerned. "It's a little too late for that. Don't you think?"

"Victor, this new version of the script is the bloodiest, most violent thing I've ever written.

But I got rid of it. I found a local cemetery and buried it."

That was a lot for Victor to take in. He imagined what that must have looked like. Full moon. Pouring rain. Lightning. Maniacal laughter. Jimmy frantically digging a grave with a shovel then tossing a script inside. Victor cleared his head and gave Jimmy some much needed advice. "You need a therapist. Fast."

Jimmy informed him, "I am! It's working."

"No, it's not, Jimmy. Try to stay focused on the film. Okay?"

Victor backed away from him. Slowly.

CHAPTER EIGHT
Love's a Slap in the Face

Even though the first day of shooting was a bust, Victor's Bar and Grill was still open for the cast and crew. All drinks and food were on Victor as part of the deal. When Scott and Laura walked in, some film crew members made room for them at the bar next to Ricky and Alison. Others weren't as nice and gave her looks that could kill.

Laura beelined right to Ricky and Alison and stomped her feet all the way. Once she reached them, she flicked Ricky's ear and he spilled his beer.

He yelled, "Hey! What was that for?!"

"You've been in here drinking the whole time?!"

Alison went around to the other side of the bar, wiped up the mess and poured another beer for him.

Ricky was fired up. "Yeah! So?"

Laura filled him in. "Well, while you were in here, I was chased with a knife and had rocks thrown at me!"

Scott sort of agreed and said, "Something like that."

Alison shook her head and laughed as she sat back down next to Ricky. "Of course. Why am I not surprised?"

Laura took offense. "What is your problem, bitch?"

Ricky gently pushed Laura away and said, "Do you mind? Alison and I were in the middle of a really deep conversation." Scott was enjoying the sibling antics. Technically, Alison started that one, but he was amused that he didn't have to defend his sister from Laura anymore. Ricky was doing just fine.

Laura looked back and forth at Ricky and Alison. She pulled up a stool and sat directly between them. Scott wasn't sure if she was trying to split them up or join the conversation, so he quietly stood behind Laura and took his bodyguard stance.

Laura complained, "Now I have to have a drink. Are you happy now? Ten days of sobriety and you ruined it."

Scott listened intently. She had to be kidding.

Ricky called her out on it. "I thought it was a month!"

"Six days. Five. Maybe three." Laura wasn't sure.

"Don't blame me for this," Ricky said.

Laura placed an order with Alison. "I'll have a double shot of vodka."

Alison looked to Scott, who was still trying to assess the situation. Alison didn't want to serve Laura without his blessing.

Scott intervened and said, "Laura, I don't think that's a good..."

Laura cut him off. "Don't tell me what I can and cannot do! I'm having a bad day and I'm not even in LA." Scott tried to process this. He thought about his job description. Victor only said to keep Laura out of trouble. He didn't say anything about drinking, or maybe Victor assumed that Scott knew better. As long as he kept her under control and within sight at all times, Scott was confident there wouldn't be an issue. He glanced at Laura and she seemed to be waiting for his response. He agreed it was a tough, stressful day for both of them. Laura mouthed the word, "Please?"

Scott caved and gave a nod of approval to Alison who fetched the vodka. Laura quickly downed the shot and said, "Fill me back up, please?"

Alison smiled. "Wow. You actually have some manners."

"So now I'm a bitch for being nice?"

Alison shrugged her shoulders as Ricky told Scott, "You're going to earn your paycheck tonight, bro. Watch out."

Alison refilled the shot glass again, and again and again. It was a long night indeed, but it was filled with laughs, smiles and bad jokes. Laura seemed to warm up to Scott and moved closer to him as the night grew on. She rested her head on his shoulder, whispered in his ear, scratched his back and even tickled him at one point. Scott seemed to forget how much they couldn't stand each other just days earlier.

Finally, many hours, beers and shots later, it was closing time, even though the bar wasn't technically open. Everyone went separate ways and Scott led Laura outside arm in arm.

The car ride seemed instantaneous. When they arrived at the hotel, Scott opened the door to her room and she hurried inside. She playfully waved at Scott who remained in the hallway.

Laura slurred her words. "Aren't you coming in?"

"No, I think I'm going to..."

Before Scott could give an answer, Laura dragged him into the room and locked the door behind them. Laura stumbled as she approached Scott, but regained her balance and shoved him onto the bed.

Laura confessed, "I have to admit, Scott. When we first met? I hated you. Hated-hated-hated you."

"I think the feeling was mutual," Scott countered without missing a beat.

Laura's mouth hung wide open, her feelings obviously hurt.

Scott wondered how they managed to get this far. After all, just days earlier, they were at each other's throats. He could tell that Laura was trying to seduce him. It turned him on, but the timing was wrong. He wondered if she would have acted like this if she was sober.

Scott wasn't trying to upset her, just play along. "But you're not so bad after all."

Laura quickly smiled. "Awww."

"You're all right...for a movie star," Scott added.

Laura sat down on the bed very close to him. Their legs rubbed against each other and Scott went from comfortable to nervous in a matter of seconds.

Laura told him, "I always wanted to date a regular guy, but they get intimidated by me. It never works. I've been stuck dating actors for years. I'm so tired of it."

Scott tried his best to make her feel better. "Most girls would trade places with you in a heartbeat."

"You have no idea what my life is like. It's fun for a while, but gets old real fast."

Laura's head swayed, and her eyes got heavy.

Scott knew where they were headed and tried to take control. "Well, I'm glad you got the part in the movie. I'm having a great time."

Laura placed her hand on Scott's leg. "Thanks for taking the job. You treat me different than other guys."

That was all he needed to hear. As much as he was enjoying the compliments and Laura's transparent seduction, he knew what he had to do. This was the moment, the crossroads. Scott took the bait by entering the room with her. Now she was trying to reel him in. Scott either had to sleep with her or get out of there fast.

Scott started to stand up. "I think I better..."

Laura got a second wind of strength and grabbed his arm. "No! Don't go!"

Scott knew what would happen if he stayed, so he argued, "It's getting late and..."

Laura cut him off again, this time by planting a kiss on his lips. Scott surprised Laura by pulling away from her.

"Laura, you're drunk," he said.

She tried to kiss him again, but Scott kept backing off. As much as he wanted to kiss her, it was wrong. As a bartender, he often resisted the advances of intoxicated customers, so that's exactly what he did here. It was the right thing to do.

Much louder, he reasserted, "You're drunk!"

Laura thought for a moment, and then slapped Scott across the face as hard as she could.

She screamed, "Get out!"

Scott pleaded, "I'm sorry!"

"I hate you! Get out of my room!"

He climbed off the bed and headed for the door. Laura pushed him out of the room and slammed the door in his face. He stared at the closed door for a few moments. He heard Laura screaming inside, followed by the sound of things being thrown around the room and glass breaking.

Scott was about to knock, but lowered his head and shuffled toward his own room. How did he let such a fun night end like this? Regardless, he knew the situation could only be dealt with in the morning, which came all too fast with very little sleep.

~ * ~

The next morning, Laura woke up to a bleary world of brightness. She had passed out half-naked on her bed with no covers. She had slept well, but was now paying the price of a nasty hangover. The sunshine coming through the windows revealed the hotel room to be completely trashed.

Laura heard the pounding on the door along with the ringing of her cell phone, but she ignored it. She listened to Scott's voice through the door.

"You're going to be late to the set if you don't get up!"

Laura looked at the clock and quickly jumped out of bed. She grabbed her forehead in pain, squinted her eyes and surveyed the damage to the room. She didn't remember trashing it, but that didn't matter. It wasn't the first time. She pulled herself together the best she could and walked right past Scott as she exited her room. She kept herself a good distance ahead of him on the walk to the car.

She put on a tough exterior, but the reality was that she was terribly embarrassed. She had a tendency to ruin things just when they were going well. Scott was growing on her and she didn't know how to deal with it. More than anything, she was mad at herself.

~ * ~

As Scott drove Laura to the set, it was complete silence the whole ride. If he turned on the radio, she turned it off. Scott wanted to talk about the night before, but didn't know how to start the conversation. He never once second guessed his decision to resist her, but was worried she didn't understand why. Even though they weren't even a couple, Scott's heart ached, just like it did whenever he blew a first date. He didn't think he would get another chance.

As Laura and Scott walked into the bar, they were greeted with cameras, lights, boom mics, and of course, a frantic film crew. The bar was fully converted into a movie set. Scott was somewhat distracted by the Hollywood decor, but still noticed that Laura strayed away from him. He looked around and saw there were more people hanging around than normal. Matt brought an entire entourage of his friends and co-stars from his prank show. They were all gathered at a table and whispered to each other. Scott watched as Laura passed by them, but then suddenly and without warning, she was pelted in the face with a water balloon.

Laura froze as Scott immediately rushed to her side. Some of Matt's friends erupted into laughter while others played it cool. Scott was still reeling from the night before, so he needed

Laura to prompt him back into work mode and that's exactly what she did. "Are you going to do something about this?!" she asked.

Scott looked over at Matt, then back at Laura and advised, "Let it go. It's a joke."

She wiped her face then sniffed her hand and shouted, "It was filled with beer!"

Laura pushed Scott aside and stood in front of Matt and his entourage.

She screamed, "Who threw it?"

Matt and the others looked around the room and at each other with confused faces.

Laura demanded an answer. "Who did this?!"

Laura turned to Scott and slapped him across the face. If that wasn't enough, she slapped him a second time.

He asked, "What did I do?!"

"Nothing! You did absolutely nothing! Again!"

After a long silence, Laura headed toward the makeup girl on the other side of the bar, who immediately picked balloon pieces from her hair, face and shirt. Matt's entourage pointed and laughed as Scott chased after Laura.

While Laura sat in the makeup chair, Scott collected his thoughts by the window. As the handprint from Laura's double slap slowly disappeared, Scott felt like everyone was staring at him. His stomach was already in knots over her and she made it worse by slapping him in front of everyone on the first day. He didn't know how he was going to survive thirty days of this.

As he gazed out the window, he noticed Jimmy Corn stepping out of his trailer. Jimmy was wearing a full karate uniform tied with a black belt. He held a metal Chinese star in front of him, kissed it, and then placed it in the pocket of his uniform. Scott worried that if Laura saw this, it would send her into another panic attack, but he figured she had enough on her mind. Jimmy wasn't her biggest concern anymore.

Jimmy made his way into the bar and took a seat in the director's chair with his name on the back of it. Jimmy was unusually relaxed, especially considering what he was wearing. Laura didn't seem to care either, just as Scott expected.

Once Laura was cleaned up, the shoot began and the crew got the actors ready and in their places for the first scene. Matt sat at the bar among lots of extras while Laura was stationed off camera.

Scott stood near the back of the set with Alison and Ricky. This was it. The first scene of

Pretty Ugly with Matt and Laura. Scott looked around the room. Everyone seemed excited and nervous at the same time as Jimmy shouted, "Action!"

Laura quickly entered the scene and placed drinks in front of random extras. She poured one for Matt, but once it was full, she spilled it all over him.

Alison laughed out loud and was met with angry looks from the crew, as well as Victor and Jimmy. Scott jabbed her with his elbow. Alison whispered, "I taught her that."

Jimmy told Matt and Laura, "Don't stop! Keep going!"

Laura paused, grabbed a rag and wiped up the mess. She also rubbed Matt's shirt and asked, "What's your name?"

Matt responded with his character name, "Ace."

"Well, Ace, the rest of your drinks are on me."

Laura ran her hand through his hair and poured him another beer. They smiled at each other.

Jimmy yelled, "Cut!"

Both of their smiles instantly disappeared. Matt stood up and looked down at his drenched shirt and pants.

"What the...? You did that on purpose!"

"I think I got my line wrong. Let me try that again." Laura threw herself back in the scene and asked, "All drinks are on you?"

Scott watched Laura fight back a smile, but it was there. He saw it. He was proud of her for standing her ground and pushing back.

Jimmy stepped between them as he tightened the belt on his karate outfit. "That's not how I wrote the scene, but I liked it. I might use that take. Let's do it again, but this time, try not to spill his beer, okay Laura?"

Once Jimmy walked away, Matt warned Laura, "It's on now."

Laura laughed. "Whatever. Bring it."

"Don't worry. I will," Matt promised.

The makeup girl and a set designer tended to Matt. They used a hair dryer to get rid of the wet spot as Laura and the rest of the crew got ready for a second take, and a third, and a fourth. It was a long day. When the shoot was over, Laura consulted with Jimmy and a few crew members, and then walked out to the car.

As Scott drove, Laura leaned her head on the passenger window and stared blankly into the night. Once again, no talking, no radio, just another uncomfortable silence.

Scott looked back and forth between Laura and the road. "How do you feel about the first day?"

Laura ignored him.

"Laura?"

No response.

"We're still not talking?"

Again, no response. It was another long car ride. Scott couldn't wait to go to bed and start fresh in the morning. He suspected some sleep would help Laura, too. She entered her hotel room and slammed the door. Scott didn't want to let her out of his sight, so he grabbed a chair near the elevator and stayed in the hallway.

CHAPTER NINE
When Your Walls Come Down

Laura sat in her hotel room all alone. She paced around as she constantly watched her phone. She was terribly bored and needed to do something. She was going to go crazy if she stayed there another minute.

Laura grabbed the wig and sunglasses off the table and put them on. She peeked her head out of the hotel room only to see Scott sitting in the chair over by his room. He noticed her and waved. She glared at him and growled like a wild animal ready to tear him to shreds. Who did he think he was? She was tired of being treated like a child. Laura needed to get out. She needed a plan.

Scott approached the door and attempted to calm her down. "Laura, I know you want to go out drinking, but it's a bad idea. Let's just forget about last night and start over." Laura wanted nothing to do with him and slammed the door behind her again.

Laura reached under her bed, pulled out a suitcase, opened it and rummaged through the contents. She found a small, unopened bottle of vodka and shoved it in her purse.

She walked out her balcony door and looked down into the parking lot. She was too high to jump down, but she had an idea.

At the edge of the railing, she peered down at the balcony below. She looked around at the other balconies of the hotel to make sure nobody was watching.

She dialed a number on her cell phone. Ricky answered on the other end. "Hello?"

Laura was never happier to hear his voice. "Ricky? Where are you?"

"I'm at the bar with Alison," he replied.

"You're with his sister again? At that stupid bar? What are you trying to do with her?"

Ricky put her in her place. "Mind your own business! What is your problem with her anyway?"

"Ugh! Whatever! Maybe you can help her finger paint her face."

Laura angrily hung up the phone, but it didn't matter. Ricky hung up on his end first. Laura was on her own. All she knew was that she had to get out of there, no matter what it took. She swung her leg over the railing and balanced herself on the outside ledge. She froze in fear and looked nervously at the distance below her. A fall had the potential to seriously injure her, even possibly kill her.

She took a deep breath, and then carefully lowered herself until she was dangling from the ledge. She clung to the concrete with her hands, her legs just six feet from the next balcony beneath her.

She let go and landed perfectly. She was proud of herself. Mission accomplished. She laughed as she banged on the door of the random hotel room. An older woman answered and was surprised and scared at the same time. Even without the wig and sunglasses, the woman was probably too old to recognize her. Laura simply explained that she was locked out of her room and was trying to climb up. The woman let her exit through her front door and just like that Laura was free. She held her middle finger up to the ceiling above her.

Even though Scott couldn't hear her, she yelled, "Loser!"

Laura danced her way down the hallway to the elevator. She knew Scott would be sitting outside her room all night with no clue that she secretly escaped. Except for when she returned, but she wasn't worried about that.

~ * ~

Over at the bar, Ricky complained to Alison about Laura's phone call. "I don't understand why she can't just chill out and focus on the movie."

The bar was still set up for filming. All the equipment was right where the crew left it, but they were closed to the public and Alison and Ricky were the only ones there. They sat so close to each other that it looked like Alison was playfully sitting on his lap. Unlike Scott, Alison wasn't nervous around movie stars. She was relaxed and comfortable around Ricky, confident in her own skin.

Alison confessed, "You're nothing like I expected."

Ricky was curious and asked, "What were you expecting?"

"I don't know. Whenever I see you on TV, you're always obnoxious. Pulling stunts and pranks, kid stuff. Like that Matt London guy in the movie."

Ricky explained, "That's what Hollywood does to people like me. Now I have a reputation to keep."

"Not if you don't want to," Alison argued.

"When there's no cameras or people around, I'm the most boring guy you'll ever meet."

Alison countered, "That's not true. If I thought you were boring, I wouldn't be sitting here with you, now would I?"

She refilled their beers as they laughed, smiled and flirted into the night. As time went by, they somehow managed to move closer together.

Alison was never one to hold anything back and inquired, "So why is your sister such a bitch?"

Ricky seemed like he had endured this conversation before with many other people and replied, "She's not always like that."

Alison didn't believe him. "So it's all an act? Just like you?"

"No, she's for real sometimes, but she never found her groove after *My Little Robot*."

"But everyone loved that show and she did the cutest dance ever," Alison admitted.

Ricky got slightly defensive of Laura. "She doesn't want to be remembered for that, and she hates talking about her small part on my Venice Beach show."

"I don't get it. Why? Everyone loved her, and those shows were so popular."

Ricky continued, "Laura's weird about our dad. She's tired of getting parts because he's producing or because of who he knows. She wants to do her own thing."

Alison pieced it all together. Everything was starting to make sense. "That's what this *Pretty*

Ugly movie's all about? She's finally separating herself from her father?"

Ricky looked away and Alison immediately knew he was hiding a secret as he confided, "Not exactly."

"What do you mean?"

Ricky asked, "Can you keep a secret?"

"Of course," Alison promised.

Ricky just blurted it out. "There are no outside investors. Our dad's behind the whole thing."

Alison didn't know what to say. For the first time, she felt a little bit of compassion for Laura.

Ricky continued, "Jimmy Corn couldn't get this movie made because it's not what his fans want to see. So my dad cut a deal with Victor, who cut a deal with Jimmy, and so on, and so on. Shannon Green was never even involved. It was just part of the act."

Alison heard enough and felt someone needed to stick up for Laura. "That is so wrong."

Ricky explained, "In fact, my dad's the one that made Victor hire a babysitter. I'm the backup plan in case your brother can't handle her. That's the only reason I'm here."

Alison asked, "Why would your father go through all this trouble?"

"Hey, she's daddy's little girl. Her career's been in trouble for years and then Tony Steel released a snippet of a sex tape and threatened to leak the whole thing. It all just snowballed from there."

Alison demanded, "You have to tell her."

Ricky pointed out, "What good would that do? So far everything's working."

Alison pleaded with him. "How would you like it if the roles were reversed? If this was being done to you?" Alison was somewhat disappointed in Ricky, but didn't want to let it ruin the night.

Alison finished her drink as fast she could. "We're closed. Let's get out of here."

~ * ~

On the other side of town, Laura's car swerved recklessly into opposing traffic. After a chorus of beeps, she moved back into her lane, nearly cutting off another car in the process.

Laura took a long swig from the bottle of vodka, which was nearly empty. Her head swayed a bit and she spilled some alcohol on her shirt and the car seat while she fought a nasty bout of the hiccups.

The car sideswiped a guardrail, but that didn't slow her down. It only made her drive faster.

Laura balanced the steering wheel with her legs as she sipped the final drops of the vodka. She rolled down the window and was about to toss out the empty bottle and SMASH!

Both of the front air bags deployed and the windshield shattered. The impact locked her seatbelt into place and the vodka bottle fell to the floor.

Laura was dazed and in shock. She was definitely knocked unconscious, but couldn't tell if it was for seconds, minutes or hours. She lifted her head up and tried to look out the windshield, but the bent hood was blocking her view. She saw steam seeping into the car and smelled the antifreeze to go with it. She could hear fluids dripping underneath her.

She moved the airbag out of her way and looked at her shaking arms. She opened and closed her hands. They were okay. She reached and felt her legs after wiggling them. They definitely weren't broken. The rearview mirror was hanging by a thread on a piece of glass, so she looked at her face. Somehow, not a scratch. She let out a sigh of relief. She did see pieces of glass in her hair and picked them out.

Laura had been in her fair share of fender benders over the years, but nothing like this. She was truly frightened.

She unbuckled her seatbelt and climbed out of the car to see that it was wrapped around a tree. She saw headlights headed her way, panicked and ran down the road, leaving everything behind.

~ * ~

Back at the hotel, Scott frantically paced around Laura's door. Her room was quiet for too long. He doubted she was asleep and was worried that she was drinking inside, or worse yet, that she had managed to harm herself. How would he explain this to Victor? To Dennis? Then he saw Laura coming down the hallway toward him. He felt relieved until it sank in she'd got one over on him and wondered how she snuck out.

When she reached him, he knew something was off. She was disheveled, out of breath and clearly drunk.

Scott felt compelled to ask her anyway, "Did you really have to sneak out just so you could drink?"

Laura was speechless as she opened her door. Scott followed her in. He noticed she was trembling and helped her sit down on a chair.

She looked him right in the eye and said, "I'm in so much trouble."

"Calm down. What happened?"

Laura didn't know where to begin. "The car..."

"You were driving?"

"I missed the turn," Laura added.

Scott raised his voice. "What do you mean you missed the turn?"

Laura simply stated, "I need another rental car."

Scott saw everything slipping away from him. The job. The money. The bar. He let Laura out of his sight and she got into exactly the kind of trouble he was hired to prevent. He screwed up and he knew it. As these thoughts raced through his head, and as bad as things looked, he realized he had to make everything better for Laura.

He asked, "How did you get here?"

"I walked," Laura answered.

Just when he thought it couldn't get worse, it did. "Please tell me you didn't leave the scene of an accident."

She argued, "I didn't know what to do. I was scared."

Knock. Knock. Knock. The banging on the door startled them both as they looked at each other. Laura was overcome with fear as Scott tiptoed to the door and looked through the peephole.

Scott whispered, "I think it's a cop."

Laura froze, unsure what to do as Scott thought for a moment. The knocks continued.

He quietly instructed her, "Get undressed and jump into bed like you were sleeping."

Laura disappeared into the bedroom while Scott calmly opened the door. A detective flashed a badge as Scott pretended to be confused.

Scott asked, "Can I help you?"

The detective tried to peer around Scott as he said, "I'm looking for Laura Summer. Is she here?"

Scott matter-of-factly replied, "She's sleeping. I don't want to wake her if I don't need to. Is there a problem?"

The detective asked, "May I come in?"

"Sure," Scott answered.

The detective stepped inside and scanned the room. "I'm going to need her to come down to the station. Could you wake her up, please?"

Scott took a deep breath and said, "That won't be necessary. I know why you're here."

"So you know she was involved in a car accident tonight and fled the scene?"

"No, she wasn't. It was me. I'm her driver. She went to bed early, so I snuck out with her car. I'm the one who crashed it. I was scared and I didn't want her to know, so I ran."

The detective responded, "I appreciate your honesty, but I'm going to have to place you under arrest."

Scott turned around and the detective handcuffed him. Laura came out of her bedroom in a bra and panties and rubbed her eyes as if she just woke up.

Laura saw the handcuffs on Scott and quickly asked, "What's going on?"

Without the detective seeing, Scott winked at Laura.

The detective informed her, "Your driver was involved in a hit and run accident with your vehicle. He's spending the night in jail."

Laura angrily stepped up to Scott and slapped him across the face. Scott never doubted her acting or slapping skills. He wasn't making this sacrifice for the bar. He was doing it for Laura.

"We also found an open bottle of vodka in the car. We take drinking and driving very seriously in this town."

Laura wound up to slap Scott again. He looked into her eyes, then down at the handcuffs, and his heart sank down to his knees. He closed his eyes and braced himself for the second slap, but it didn't come. Laura stood completely still, like she was frozen.

As Scott was escorted out of the room, the detective turned to Laura and said, "Miss Summer, you're going to need another car, and another driver."

~ * ~

Meanwhile, Ricky and Alison continued their conversation in her car. "No wonder your sister has issues," Alison said. "Why can't your dad just leave her alone?"

Ricky argued, "It's not just our dad. You should see the way our mom treats her."

Alison added, "It's the way everyone treats her."

They pulled into the driveway and Ricky asked, "So this is your place?"

"Yeah, but it's pretty small compared to what you're used to."

When they entered the house, Ricky looked around at the various paintings hanging on the wall. "You painted all this stuff?"

Alison answered, "I was in college for art. I drew the new design of the bar for when Scott takes over."

Ricky asked, "What's he naming it?"

"What else? Scott's Bar and Grill. He's so predictable."

Ricky looked closer at all the detail in the sketch. "I wish I could draw like that."

Alison smiled. "You want to see some more?"

"Sure," he replied.

Alison led Ricky upstairs.

~ * ~

The next morning, Laura arrived at the police station sporting her wig and sunglasses. She waited patiently in the lobby. She barely slept and had a long time to think. Her heart ached for Scott. She deserved to be sitting in jail, not him. No one had ever taken the fall for her like that before. Tony Steel definitely wouldn't. In fact, he would have thrown her under the bus. She felt like someone actually cared about her for once.

Finally, a police officer guided Scott into the room, removed the handcuffs and released him to Laura.

They waited for the officer to leave them alone.

Laura immediately asked, "Why did you do that?"

Scott played it down. "Hey, I signed up for this, right? It's my job. That's what I'm being paid for."

Laura argued, "No, you didn't sign up for this. I'll get you the best lawyer. I'll cover everything."

Scott looked around. "How did you get here?"

Laura took Scott by the hand and led him out of the police station where a limousine waited for them.

Scott laughed and asked, "A limo?"

"We'll get another rental car later. I owe you big time, so I'm taking you out."

Scott stopped and looked at his watch. "Wait. Why aren't you on the set?"

Laura shrugged it off like it was no big deal. "I told them I had food poisoning."

Scott seemed more concerned about it than she was. "Why did you do that? You're already on thin ice with them."

Laura rationalized, "I didn't have much of a choice. I couldn't let you sit in jail all day."

"But they were just about to release me," Scott told her.

Laura added, "It doesn't matter because I made plans for us anyway."

Scott was confused. "Plans?"

The chauffeur opened the limo door for them. Inside, Scott squirmed around and tried to get comfortable. He opened and closed windows and pressed various buttons. Laura could tell this was his first ride in a limo. She enjoyed watching him have fun.

Scott looked over at her and said, "If you insist that you owe me, then stop at my house."

Laura asked, "Why?"

He explained, "I want you to apologize to my sister. Can you at least do that for me?"

Laura shook her head. She never apologized to anyone in her life except her father. She never even told her mom or brother she was sorry for anything. Ever. She couldn't imagine apologizing to anyone else, let alone Alison.

Her instinctive response was, "Are you crazy? Hell no! I'm not..."

Laura stopped herself. Scott just spent the night in jail for her, so she went along with the request, but intended to figure something out when the moment came.

Laura creatively agreed, "I want to see where you live anyway."

"My house is probably about as big as your living room," Scott humbly admitted.

Scott climbed up to the chauffeur's window and gave him directions and the limousine did a U-turn.

After a short drive, the limo came to a stop in front of the suburban brick home. The chauffeur opened the door and Scott and Laura hopped out. They playfully ran up the sidewalk.

Scott jokingly bragged, "This is it."

Scott was right. It was nothing compared to what Laura was used to, but it had a charm to it that she had never seen before. Laura told him, "I like it. It's cute."

"I bought it from my parents about five years ago. My sister was already living here so she kind of came with the house."

Scott opened the front door for her. The first thing Laura noticed was all the artwork on the wall. "Wow, I didn't know you were into art."

"Not me. My sister is. It's all hers. She painted them."

Laura was surprised and could only get out the word, "Oh." She saw a raw talent in Alison that she never would have guessed she had. The paintings were among the best she ever laid eyes on. Her opinion of Alison started to change even more.

Out of nowhere, a cat came out to greet them. Laura loved cats and knelt down to pet the orange and white fur ball.

"Awww. What's your cat's name?"

"Wilber," Scott answered. "Best cat ever. And he's a famous YouTube cat too."

Laura replied, "I have a cat named Criss, and sorry, but he's the best cat ever."

Scott didn't agree, but chose not to argue the point. He turned back to the artwork and continued, "There's a special drawing that I want to show you."

They thought they were alone, but suddenly heard footsteps.

Scott called out, "Alison?"

Laura was dumbfounded at the sight before them. Ricky was in his boxers with no shirt. She groaned, "Ricky?"

Ricky was more concerned about Laura though. "Laura? Are you okay? They shut production down today. They said you were sick. Mom's on her way from LA. Everyone's worried about you."

"I'm fine," she insisted.

Alison appeared in the doorway, wearing only an oversized t-shirt.

"Hi, Scott."

It was officially awkward. Over the years, Laura had met many of Ricky's conquests and basically ignored every single one of them like they didn't even exist, but that streak was over. Not only did she have to acknowledge Alison, but somehow had to muster up the strength to apologize to her. To top it off, Alison was standing before her in a t-shirt and panties. It felt like a bad dream and she just wanted to wake up.

Alison managed to squeak out, "Hi, Laura."

Laura immediately responded, "Hi, Alison."

Scott elbowed Laura and whispered, "Let's get out of here. We can do this another time." Scott was clearly as uncomfortable as Laura was.

Laura was relieved inside, more so about postponing the apology. She was prepared to tell Alison she was sorry, but felt pressured into saying it. While Laura sincerely felt bad about the way she treated Scott's sister, she didn't feel it warranted words.

They clearly interrupted something and neither of them wanted to stick around any longer than necessary. Laura already saw way more than she wanted and added, "Well, okay then, we're going to leave now so you two can be alone."

Ricky asked, "Are we going to see you guys on set tomorrow?"

Scott answered, "That's the plan."

Laura assured him with her trademark attitude, "I'm the star. Remember?"

Ricky laughed. "I know. Just checking. They're worried about you is all. Mom, Victor, Jimmy. Even Matt, I think."

"Don't worry about me. I'll be there," Laura insisted. She looked at Scott and asked, "You'll make sure I'm on time, right?"

"Of course."

Scott looked around the room and saw a folded-up piece of paper sitting on the shelf. His eyes lit up as he grabbed it and placed it in his wallet.

Laura pulled Scott back outside. Alison waved at them as they left.

Inside the limo, Scott and Laura looked at each other. Both were stunned.

Scott remarked, "Wow. That was weird."

Laura agreed. "Yeah, let's forget we even saw that."

Scott asked, "So where are you taking me?"

Laura smiled as she climbed to the chauffeur's window and asked, "Is there a mall around here?"

CHAPTER TEN
King of Hearts

I t was like a scene right out of a cheesy eighties movie. They walked around the mall like a couple, sometimes holding hands. Nobody noticed them because of Laura's wig and sunglasses.

They shopped in various high-end department stores as Laura helped Scott pick out new clothes. She made him try on many different outfits. Most guys would have been bored. Scott felt like he was being treated like a movie star, and he loved every second of it. This was the most attention a girl had given him in years. His confidence was all over his face, his voice and his stride.

Outside the dressing rooms, they talked and laughed as though they had been dating for years. Scott posed in front of the mirrors as Laura cheered him on.

Laura even brought him into a women's lingerie shop. Scott was a good sport, especially when Laura quietly pulled him into a dressing room when no one was looking. She made him turn around while she tried some bras on, but always asked his opinion on each one. This part was the only struggle for Scott and made him somewhat shy, but he played along.

Later, they shared a small ice cream cone in the food court. They never finished it because Laura playfully smeared the ice cream in his face. He got most of it off with a napkin. What he missed, Laura licked off with her tongue. Scott knew where the day was headed, and could tell that even Laura was nervous.

Next, she took Scott for a haircut inside the mall's barbershop. She whispered instructions into the barber's ear. Scott closed his eyes during the haircut, but when he opened them and looked in the mirror, he was pleasantly surprised.

They even took instant pictures inside an old photo booth and preserved the moment. Scott couldn't stop staring at the pictures. He kept wondering if this was really happening to him.

By the time they walked out of the mall, Scott looked like a completely different person. They loaded all the bags into the limo and cuddled in the back seat until they reached their next destination, a fancy restaurant.

They sat in a private, candlelit corner, with Scott all decked out in his new clothes and Laura still wearing her wig. They sat across from each other and held hands, as they sipped on glasses of wine. The ball was in Scott's court. He would be content to sit there and stare into her eyes all day, but knew she would eventually lose interest. He had to say something meaningful in that moment and struggled to find the right words. He wouldn't get this chance again and had to move quickly, as they were already in the middle of a long, but comfortable silence.

Scott gathered his thoughts the best he could and proclaimed, "This has probably been one of the best days of my life, which is amazing, considering I spent the night in jail. Thank you."

Laura corrected him. "No. Thank you." She motioned for the waiter to top off their wine glasses.

Scott asked, "Are you trying to get me drunk?"

"Maybe. Neither one of us has to drive. I've got the limo all night."

Scott pulled the folded up piece of paper out of his wallet. He opened it and handed it to Laura.

"Here's that drawing I was telling you about at my house earlier. My sister drew it for me."

Laura looked at the drawing. It was a prototype of the new exterior of the bar with a sign that read, Scott's Bar and Grill.

"That's nice. Your sister's a really good artist," Laura admitted.

"Are you mad she's dating Ricky?" Scott asked.

Laura quipped, "Would she be mad if I was dating you?"

Scott was caught off guard. His heart raced as his eyes grew wide. His whole body felt numb as if someone just told him he won the lottery. He had to make sure he heard her right. He asked Laura to clarify. "We're dating?"

Laura surprised him with, "I'm breaking up with Tony."

Scott had the sudden urge to jump up and down and dance around the room, but kept it all inside and played it cool. The last thing he wanted to do was scare Laura off, but he couldn't believe she was breaking up with Tony to be with him.

Laura added, "I have to do it with him in person though. If I did it over the phone, he'd be on the next flight out of Budapest and trust me, we don't want him showing up here. Tony would kill you. And me. Literally."

Scott asked, "So what does that mean for us? Right now?"

"Whatever you want it to mean," Laura replied. "Tony and I have been in a dead relationship for a long time. He just refuses to admit it. As far as I'm concerned, we're done. It's over."

A slow song started to play from the jukebox. Laura jumped out of her chair and screamed, "I love this song. Will you dance with me?"

Laura grabbed Scott by the hand and pulled him up from his seat. Scott resisted. "No, you go ahead."

Laura argued, "I can't slow dance by myself. Who does that?"

She removed her wig and her blonde hair cascaded down her back.

Scott looked around, surprised that she took it off. "What are you doing?"

Laura held out her hand. "Now will you dance with me? Please?"

Scott couldn't resist anymore. Laura led him to a secluded area. She placed her arms over Scott as he reached around her waist and they began to dance.

He whispered, "Why did you take the wig off?"

"I have nothing to hide anymore."

"But what if someone sees us?"

Laura ignored the question and made the first move and inched her lips closer to Scott's. Finally, they stopped dancing and kissed for what seemed the entire song, and into the next. They were oblivious to everything around them.

Once they returned to the table, they quickly took care of the tab and left arm in arm. Scott was normally used to long car rides home, but on this night, he wished he could slow down time. Laura was all over him in the backseat of the limo and her hands wandered to places that he wasn't used to.

When they arrived at the hotel, Laura couldn't open her door fast enough. She pulled Scott inside and practically threw him onto the bed. He watched as she started to undress. Before he knew it, she was down to her bra and panties. Scott trembled in anticipation of what came next. He couldn't believe this was happening. Scott had gone through many girlfriends through his teen years and into his twenties. He experienced so many emotions in each relationship that he was prepared for anything. But he wasn't prepared for this. He never had these kinds of strange, tingling sensations for a girl before. This was better than his first kiss. Better than when he had lost his virginity. And it had nothing to do with her being a celebrity. He was in love.

As Laura pranced across the room, she unfastened her bra and quickly covered her breasts with one arm. She backed herself up against the wall and suddenly the room went pitch black.

Scott panicked. Did a light bulb die? A fuse blow? Or was there a power outage? How could this happen to him during such a hot, intense moment?

He instinctively reached for the bedside lamp, pulled the chain and the room lit up. He didn't even have a chance to lay eyes on Laura again as she screamed, "No! Turn it off!"

He immediately turned the lamp off and they were back in the dark. Laura calmly added, "I like the lights off."

"Why?" Scott asked.

"Why does it matter?" Laura countered.

She climbed onto the bed and began kissing him again. And with that, Scott accepted the darkness. It didn't matter anyway. He didn't need to see her. He even closed his eyes. He could see her just fine, at least in his own mind.

CHAPTER ELEVEN
Tough Love

Scott and Laura faced each other on her bed, naked under the blanket. Laura was still sleeping and her eyes were closed. Scott just watched her, still in disbelief. Then suddenly, Laura opened one eye. Scott smiled at her and ran his hand through her hair. He just woke up next to a movie star. He felt reinvigorated and full of energy, eager to start the day and see where this new path took him.

Out of nowhere, Laura grabbed the blanket to fully cover herself. She jumped off the bed and screamed, "What are you doing in here?"

"Huh?" was all Scott could get out.

Laura cringed, "Did we?"

Not only was Scott confused, he was crushed. His recollection of the night was a very intimate one. He didn't think she was drunk. He asked, "You don't remember?"

Laura backed away and stated, "I remember drinking, and dancing, but after that, I don't know. I can't remember."

Scott climbed out of bed and quickly put his clothes back on. "I'm sorry. I better go."

Laura seemed angrier with herself than at Scott as she walked over to his side of the bed. "Oh my god. I'm such a slut."

He tried to get dressed even faster as she stood right in front of him.

Laura demanded, "How could you take advantage of me like that?"

Once his pants were buckled, he stopped and looked right at her.

Scott never saw this coming and just wanted to disappear. He didn't have an explanation. There were no words he could string together that could fix this. It was over. He simply muttered, "Laura, I..."

Without warning, Laura pushed Scott back onto the bed and kissed him, but only briefly because she couldn't stop herself from laughing.

"Of course I remember. Gotcha!"

Scott sighed in relief. "Okay, you got me. That was good."

Laura bragged, "I'm a hell of an actress, aren't I?"

Scott's stomach felt like he just stepped off the world's tallest roller coaster. He wasn't used to going from one emotional extreme to another. Needless to say, he was relieved. "I never said you weren't, but you didn't have to do that."

"Haven't you ever watched any of my movies or shows?" Laura asked.

Scott thought to himself for a moment. She walked herself right into it. This was his chance, so he informed her, "Actually I was watching *My Little Robot* the other night."

He could tell she was losing interest in the conversation fast, so he went all in and said the unthinkable.

"Can you do the robot dance for me?"

Laura looked like she just saw a ghost. Her eyes widened as she ground her teeth. She took a deep breath and asked, "What did you just say to me?"

Scott replied, "I don't understand what the big deal is. You won't even do it for me?"

Scott knew he was in uncharted territory here.

Laura clenched her fists just like she had done before she clocked him the night they met. He was well aware of the risks involved in asking her to do the dance, but felt comfortable enough with her to roll the dice. Now he wished he could take it back, but it was too late. He misjudged his boundaries and crossed a line.

Just as Scott braced himself for a possible punch to the face, Laura's cell phone rang and she quickly answered and put it on speaker. "Hello?"

It was Victor, and he did not sound happy. His voice blasted through the phone, "Laura, I just want you to know it wasn't me!"

"What are you talking about?" she asked.

"You didn't hear about it yet?"

"No. What's going on?"

"Someone placed an ad in every one of the trades today and called you out."

Even thought Scott wasn't familiar with the trades, that was all he needed to hear to know it was serious.

Laura asked, "What do you mean? What does it say?"

"I faxed it to the front desk. Go down and read it yourself."

"Okay. I will. But..."

Victor's voice sounded like his patience was running thin. "Just be on time today."

Click. Victor hung up the phone. Laura looked at Scott with a blank expression as she scrambled to get dressed.

Scott asked, "What's the matter?"

"Everything," Laura replied.

She hurried out the door and told him, "Wait here!"

No matter how bad the situation was, it couldn't have come at a better time. Laura seemed to have moved on from Scott's ill-advised request for the robot dance. He made a mental note to himself not to ask her again. He considered himself lucky Victor had called.

~ * ~

Downstairs, Laura startled the desk clerk. She was barely dressed with no makeup and frizzy hair.

The desk clerk instantly recognized her. "Good morning, Miss Summer. Are you looking for a fax?"

"Yes."

"It just came in," he said as he handed her the fax.

As she read it, she gagged, ready to throw up. She held it in and looked up at the desk clerk.

"Did you read this?" she angrily asked.

With a devil's smile, he answered, "Of course not."

Laura knew he was lying, but changed the subject. "Could you tell me what room Jimmy Corn is staying in?"

"He's in room 327."

Laura hurried to the elevator with the fax clenched in her hand. When she reached the third floor, Laura banged repeatedly on the door of room 327. She waited and kept knocking. Finally, Jimmy answered the door in his bathrobe and was surprised to see her.

"Laura?"

A loud thump could be heard from within the room. Laura sniffed the air and glared at Jimmy. She knew that scent. She recognized it all too well.

"Is my mother in there?" Laura asked as she squinted her eyes. She tried to peek around Jimmy, but he wouldn't let her.

Laura argued, "I can smell her perfume from here."

She pushed past Jimmy and barged into the room. She went straight to the bed and ripped the covers back to reveal Sophia.

"Mom? What are you doing?! God!"

Laura dropped to her knees and held out the fax to Sophia. Laura fought back tears and was very careful not to cry in front of Jimmy.

"Honey, what's the matter now?" Sophia asked.

"This was published in all the trades today!"

Before Sophia even laid eyes on it, Jimmy snatched the fax out of her hand and started to read it out loud.

"An Open Letter to Laura Summer: Since filming began on *Pretty Ugly*, you have repeatedly disrupted the set with your immature behavior. Whether showing up late, or not showing up at all, you have insulted the efforts of the entire cast and crew."

Jimmy had Sophia's undivided attention as she crawled across the bed.

Laura cringed at every word.

Jimmy continued reading. "We are tired of the excuses. Yesterday, it was food poisoning. What will it be tomorrow?"

Sophia leapt off the bed, ripped the fax out of Jimmy's hand and picked up reading where he left off.

"In addition to costing the production thousands of dollars, you have turned the cast and crew against you, and are jeopardizing the quality and integrity of the film. This is your final warning before further action is taken."

Sophia became dizzy and used the fax to fan herself and said, "Oh my goodness, this could kill your career. We need to spin it."

Laura got right in Jimmy's face. If Victor didn't write it, then maybe it was Jimmy. Laura felt the need to stand up to him, especially with her mom there to back her up.

"Did you place that ad, Jimmy?"

He screamed, "No! Why would I do something like that to my own film?"

Laura added, "Victor called. He said he didn't do it either."

Sophia asked, "Then who did?"

Jimmy's whole body twitched. He was having a breakdown.

"Somebody's trying to sabotage my film! Somebody's trying to give it bad buzz!"

From under the pillow, Jimmy pulled out his Chinese star and threw it at the door. The blades stuck into the wood just under the peephole.

Sophia shielded Laura. "We're going to leave you alone, Jimmy."

Sophia put on the rest of her clothes, grabbed her purse and opened the door. As Laura stared at the Chinese star, Sophia pulled her out of the room and led her down the hallway, Laura resisted and pushed her away.

"Mommy! Why are you sleeping with the director?! You're not even in the movie!"

Sophia stopped and grabbed Laura's shoulders.

"You need to worry about yourself. You need to stay focused!"

Laura complained, "I'm ruined. Everyone in Hollywood has read that by now."

This was supposed to be her comeback and somehow she only managed to embarrass herself. No one in Hollywood would want to work with her. This was her test and she failed.

Sophia gave Laura a boost of confidence. "Let me handle this, dear. You just show up to the set. Get there early. Be a professional and give them their money's worth. Don't let them rattle you. Just be strong, okay?"

Laura nodded her head in agreement, but it was much easier said than done.

CHAPTER TWELVE
Boomerang

When Laura arrived on the set with Scott, she walked briskly past everyone and acted as if everything was fine. As she neared Matt and his entourage, she slowed down and watched their every move. They all pretended not to notice her. She followed her mother's advice and kept her head up. For Laura, this was a walk of shame. She was scared and trembling inside, but hid it well.

Once she reached her trailer, she turned to Scott and told him, "I need to lie down for a few minutes and relax. Can you wait out here and keep an eye on Matt? I don't trust him."

"Yeah, sure," Scott replied.

Once Laura slipped inside, she stood by the window and peered outside. She watched Scott grab a lawn chair and sit down outside her door. Matt and Scott waved at each other. This made Laura even more suspicious. Something didn't seem right.

Regardless, she had to mentally prepare for the day's scenes. She flopped down on the sofa, kicked her legs up and closed her eyes. Just as she nodded off, a fly landed on her nose. She felt it and swatted at her face.

Seconds later, another fly landed on her forehead. She swatted again, then opened her eyes. Once she heard the buzzing sound, she hopped off the sofa and looked around. There were hundreds of flies inside the trailer with her.

She sprinted out the door and nearly tripped over her own feet, almost knocking Scott over.

"What's wrong?" Scott asked.

She didn't stop to answer and ran right by Matt and his entourage, who all pointed and laughed.

Scott jumped out of the lawn chair and chased after her.

As she darted past Jimmy in his director's chair, he stood up and shouted, "Are you kidding me?"

Scott promised, "She'll be right back!"

Laura stopped by their new rental car. She was tired of the games, tired of the pranks. An open letter in the trades. Flies in her trailer. Laura was worried about what would come next.

As Scott approached her, she worried for the first time about what he thought of her. She waited for him to say something, but he didn't. He put his arms around her and simply gave her a hug, one that lasted for several minutes, one she wished could last the entire day. She was growing fond of his embrace and found herself thinking of him more than she would ever care to admit.

~ * ~

As they returned to the set, the entire crew was silent. Scott could tell that all attention was on Laura. He saw all the dirty looks pointed her way. Laura couldn't have noticed since she stared at the floor and avoided eye contact with everyone except for Jimmy and Matt.

The rest of the day's shoot went smooth considering the stress from all the bad publicity. Laura was a trooper and delivered her lines with poise and turned in a performance that Jimmy had to be proud of. Even Matt London looked pleasantly surprised. More important, Scott was impressed with how professionally she handled herself. He knew it must have been difficult for her to concentrate after that open letter appeared in the trades. Scott wanted to let it be as distant a memory as possible, and never mention it to her again, although he was quietly determined to find out who was responsible.

As the cast and crew dispersed, Scott suspected that Ricky and Alison were up to something. Alison distracted Scott and pulled him away from Laura. Out of the corner of his eye, he saw Ricky swoop in and take Laura outside. Scott waited for an hour by the car before they returned. Laura gave Ricky a hug before climbing into the passenger seat.

Scott tried to initiate a conversation with Laura on the drive back to the hotel, but she gave him simple, generic responses. He could tell something was bothering her.

As they pulled into the hotel parking lot, Laura raised her voice and asked, "Did you know?"

"Know what?"

"Don't play stupid with me!"

"I don't know what you're talking about," Scott insisted.

Her tone got nastier as she grilled him. "Who hired you?"

Scott was confused. "Victor. You know that."

"Oh, please. Stop lying. I know it was my father."

Scott parked the car and then looked right at her. This was the first time since they hooked up that she seemed legitimately mad at him. It scared him. This could be the end of everything.

Scott defended himself. "I have never met or talked to your father. Victor's the one who hired me."

They stared at each other for a long time. Laura was trying to gauge whether he was being honest with her or not.

Finally, she filled him in. "My father put up all the money for the film. He's behind everything, including you."

"I'm serious, Laura. I didn't know." Scott was only telling a partial truth, since technically Ricky did tell him, but not until after he was hired.

As Laura climbed out of the car, she declared, "I'm quitting the movie."

"What? You can't do that," Scott argued as he chased after her.

They picked the conversation back up in her hotel room. Laura told him, "I would have never have done this film if I knew my father was producing it."

Scott had to talk her out of it. "I know you're upset. I understand. But quitting the movie isn't going to hurt your father. It'll hurt Victor, Jimmy, Matt and all the other actors and crew members who are working hard on this film. And me. I'm a part of this too. Don't quit on them. Don't quit on me."

She looked him in the eyes and countered, "I'll sleep on it."

That was good enough for now. He knew he could finish convincing her in the morning if needed. Scott wasn't even thinking about the money or the bar anymore. It was all about Laura.

Laura continued, "I'm not even sure who's in on it and who's not. Was this all one big joke on me? You're basically the only one I trust right now."

Laura leaned her head on Scott's shoulder. As he placed his hand on her leg, their lips touched. He grabbed her hair and gently pulled her head back and kissed her neck. Laura let out a soft moan and abruptly backed away. Before Scott knew what she was doing, the lights went out and everything was pitch black again.

Moments later, he felt her return to him and he undressed her in the dark. He wondered why she insisted on turning out the lights while they had sex. He worried that she didn't want to see him in bed, that she wasn't 100% attracted to him. Or maybe it had more to do with Tony Steel and how he secretly filmed a sex tape. Or maybe she wasn't comfortable with her own body. Whatever the reason was, Scott could only hope that one of these times, Laura would trust him enough to leave a light on.

Regardless, it was time for Laura to know how he really felt. He had to tell her he loved her. Just as he started to say the words, it was as if Laura could read his mind and she covered his mouth with her hand. He only got out the word "I" and a muffled "L" sound. He took that as a sign to wait. He planned to try again on her upcoming birthday.

When they got to the set in the morning, it was almost an exact repeat of the previous day. Laura hurried past Matt's entourage, but this time, there was a big difference. Matt was not among them. Scott knew Matt was likely up to something and could feel the eyes of his entourage upon them. Scott unlocked her trailer door and let her in. Once the door was closed, she panicked and peeked out the window.

Laura was clearly concerned. "I don't know where Matt is but I don't trust him."

Scott reminded her, "You're the better person here. If he wants to play games, let him."

Laura looked around the room. "He filled my trailer with flies. Okay? That's weird. Who does that? I have every right to be nervous around him."

Scott moved furniture around and looked under some cushions. "It doesn't look like anyone was in here. Nothing to be worried about. All clear."

Laura slowly got comfortable and relaxed. She curled up on the sofa and motioned for Scott to join her. "Power nap?"

"Sure," Scott said.

He squeezed onto the sofa with her and gently kissed the back of her neck as he wrapped his arms around her. Laura fell asleep almost instantly, but Scott remained awake and on guard.

About a half-hour later, Laura woke up and looked at the clock. She climbed off the sofa and disappeared into the bathroom. Seconds later, Scott heard her scream. He jumped up from the sofa and flung the bathroom door open.

Laura was standing there with her hand over her mouth, gagging. Scott peeked inside the toilet and saw much more than he had bargained for. It was a revolting cocktail of fecal matter and vomit, coiled like a snake. He quickly pushed the flusher, but it did nothing. It was broken.

Laura screamed again as she fled the bathroom. "I can't take this anymore. I've had it!"

Scott joined her back at the sofa. He looked out the window and saw Matt's entourage was still out there.

"I'll go talk to Matt. He's probably in his trailer."

Laura nicely pushed him aside. "No! I have to handle this myself. This is personal. It won't even flush."

She stormed out of the trailer with a crazed look in her eye.

Scott honored her wishes and stayed put, but watched intently from the window. Matt's entourage saw her coming and scattered.

~ * ~

With the entourage gone, Laura marched right up to Matt's trailer and pounded relentlessly on the door. The entourage watched the action unfold from a safe distance. They were scared and amused at the same time.

Finally, Matt came to the door shirtless and in boxers and barked, "What?!"

Laura started her rant. "I'm getting sick and tired of..."

Laura stopped mid-sentence as her nose twitched. She sniffed the air. She knew that smell. Her eyes lit up as she pushed past Matt and into his trailer. She slammed the door behind her. Matt didn't even try to stop her, sporting a devious smirk. He closely watched Laura's face for a reaction and he got one.

Laura stopped at the edge of his bed and ripped the covers back to reveal Sophia in her lingerie. "Mom? What are you doing?! God!"

All Sophia could come up with was, "Darling, go back to your trailer and go over your lines."

"Mom! Why are you doing this to me?!"

Laura could somewhat understand Sophia sleeping with Victor and Jimmy, but Matt? He was the enemy. Laura was disappointed in her mother in a way that she had never been before, and there was nothing Sophia could say in her defense to make Laura forgive her.

Matt jumped into the conversation and told Laura, "Listen to your mommy like a good little girl. Can't you see we're busy?"

Laura turned to Matt and got right in his face. She almost jabbed his eye out with her finger. "I can play this game too, Matt. You're on!"

Laura made like she was going to slug him across the face, but ran her hand through her hair instead. She then turned her attention to Sophia.

"And you, Mother! You should be ashamed of yourself!"

Laura had never spoken to her like that before. Sophia was speechless as Laura kept her cool and calmly walked out the door.

Laura had no choice but to shoot the movie with Matt that day. She remained professional and worked through their scenes as if nothing happened, but was quietly plotting her revenge. Matt crossed a line and she wasn't going to let him get away with it. It appeared that Jimmy Corn and the rest of the crew had no idea of the trouble that was brewing between the two lead stars.

Later that night, as Scott and Laura cuddled in bed together, he teased, "I've got big plans for your birthday tomorrow."

Laura was curious. "What? Tell me!"

"Yeah, right. It's a surprise," Scott countered.

She wasn't expecting anything from Scott. She didn't even know how he found out it was her birthday, but it didn't matter. She was excited because her past birthdays had a tendency to end in disaster, especially the last few with Tony Steel. She was confident that this year would be different, which unfortunately reminded her of the pending break-up with Tony, so she shifted gears and got serious for a moment. "Has anyone asked you any questions about us?"

"No. Why?"

Laura informed him, "I just think it's a good idea to keep this between us...for now."

"Is that why you still keep slapping me in front of everyone?" Scott asked.

Laura tried not to laugh as she confirmed, "I don't want them to suspect anything!"

Scott agreed. "It's working."

Laura continued, "If word of us got out, Tony would show up and ruin everything. That's what he does best."

"I'm not afraid of him," Scott bragged.

Laura sternly said, "I am."

She had always been a strong woman that could hold her own, but Tony had managed to instill a new fear she had never experienced before. She had always been afraid of heights, spiders and clowns, but this was the first time she was afraid of an actual person.

"Why?" Scott asked.

"You don't want to know. I'm scared of him, Scott. You should be too. You don't know the things I've seen him do to people... and to me."

Laura needed to change the subject fast, so she sat up in the bed, grabbed the movie script and turned to one of the last pages. She claimed, "I still don't know what I'm going to do about the big crying scene on the last day."

Scott argued, "You have plenty of time to prepare for it."

"What if I choke on camera? Everyone's going to laugh at me," Laura feared. This was supposed to be her comeback. She didn't want her performance to be a late night punchline on the talk shows, or a viral video watched millions of times online.

Scott thought for a moment and explained, "Here's what you do. Think of something in your life that made you cry and put yourself back in that moment."

Laura laughed and rolled her eyes. "Give me a break. That's acting 101. Every teacher says that."

She was right, so Scott took it one step further. "No, they try to get you to think back to your childhood or some traumatic thing from your teen years. Think recent. Think of the last time you cried and why. Like when you read that fax."

"Who said I cried over the fax?"

"Whatever. You were upset though, right?"

Just the thought of it got Laura emotional. "I thought my life was over when I read that stupid fax."

"You see? There you go then. That's all you have to do."

Laura wholeheartedly asked, "Will you promise to be on the set that day? When I film that scene?"

Scott assured her, "It's my job. Don't I have to be there?"

"Yes," Laura seductively whispered. She pinned Scott to the bed and smothered him with kisses. As they rolled around in bed, Laura thought about the night before. She knew he had tried to say, 'I love you'. Little did Scott know, Laura refused to utter those three words to anyone. Never to her father, mother, Tony or any boyfriend so far in her life. She preferred to save those words for special moments in her life, to allow them to be all the more powerful and meaningful when spoken. She always wondered when that day would come. It was nothing against Scott. She was actually growing quite fond of him and considered him a candidate for breaking the spell. Only time would tell.

~ * ~

The next day on the set, Scott entered Laura's trailer with a grocery bag. He pulled out a bottle of mayonnaise. Laura grabbed it from him and danced around the trailer like a little kid with a mischievous laugh.

Scott asked, "Why the sudden craving for mayo?"

"Today's my big kissing scene with Matt. There's a rumor going around that he's planning to ram his tongue down my throat with a mouth full of garlic chunks. But I've got a surprise for him. I've seen Matt on TV. Everyone knows that he absolutely hates mayonnaise. He vomits just at the sight or smell of it. So...I'm going to have a mouthful of mayo waiting for him."

"You might ruin the scene," Scott warned.

"I don't care. It'll be worth it. I'll keep kissing him, so if he stops, that's on him. He will be so sorry he ever messed with me and had sex with my mother. How dare he!"

Laura took the bottle of mayonnaise from Scott and thanked him with a kiss. She then opened the mayo and ate a large spoonful. Scott turned away. He wasn't interested in watching her eat mayo like that.

On the set, Matt sat at the bar by himself, while Laura stood across from him. They were both in character as the crew stood by with the lights shining and boom mics pointed at them.

A production assistant closed the slate marker in front of the camera and quickly backed away. A few seconds went by.

"And...Action!" yelled Jimmy Corn.

The set was quiet. All eyes were on Matt and Laura. Scott watched intently from the back. He wanted to smile and laugh in anticipation of what was to come, but held it in.

After Laura waited a beat, she poured shots for them and delivered her lines to Matt.

"The doors are locked. It's our bar now," she said.

Matt looked in her eyes. "To us."

They raised their shot glasses.

"To us," Laura whispered back.

"Cheers," they both said in unison.

They drank the shots and Laura quickly poured another round. Their eyes locked as they stared at each other for what seemed like a lifetime.

Jimmy was visibly frustrated. He quietly moved his hands around like he was trying to tell them to hurry up, but they couldn't see him.

Laura reached out and ran her hand through Matt's hair. He basked in the moment and closed his eyes. Laura pulled him closer. Their lips almost touched, but they lingered for a moment. Then it happened: a gentle, but very passionate kiss.

Matt's entourage looked like they were laughing hysterically inside. They squirmed around and struggled to stay quiet. Jimmy was glued to the monitor as he watched a close-up of their prolonged kiss.

Moments later, Matt and Laura slowly pulled away from each other, both with sickened, forced smiles, and both waiting for a reaction from the other.

Jimmy yelled, "Cut!"

Even though the scene was over, Matt and Laura were still in the moment. Both felt like they got the best of the other, but both were struggling at the same time.

Jimmy hurried over to them while Matt's entourage couldn't hold back their laughter any longer.

Jimmy proclaimed, "That was beautiful. Let's do it again!"

Matt and Laura gave Jimmy the same blank, sad, and very sick to the stomach expression. They held themselves back from throwing up, neither wanting to let the other claim victory.

Laura looked over at Scott and smiled. He nodded and gave her a thumbs up as Matt ran to his trailer while covering his mouth.

Once filming was done for the day, Laura hurried to the car with Scott where they took turns laughing for the entire ride to the hotel.

Scott pulled up to the entrance to drop Laura off. "I'll pick you up at six," he told her.

"Please give me a hint," Laura begged.

"Nope," Scott insisted.

Laura argued, "But you're not supposed to let me out of your sight."

"I think we're beyond that now. Just make sure you're ready."

Laura assured him, "I will."

She leaned in for a kiss, but Scott backed away and reminded her, "I think you should really brush your teeth after all that."

"Oh yeah." Laura giggled and added, "But I want kisses later."

Scott agreed, "You have a deal, birthday girl."

Laura blew him a kiss as she jumped out of the car and ran inside to get ready. She felt like a teenager getting ready for the prom.

CHAPTER THIRTEEN
Heart of Chrome

Laura's hair was amazing. Her makeup complimented her red dress and diamond earrings. Absolute beauty. She was stunning. She hadn't been this excited about anything in a long time.

There was a knock at the door. Laura looked at her watch as she pulled herself away from the mirror.

"You're early," she whispered under her breath.

She smiled ear to ear as she opened the door, but quickly froze and her mouth dropped wide open. Tony Steel was standing before her. In person, he was much larger and muscular than he appeared in recent photos. He sported an all black suit with his hair slicked back into a small ponytail.

Tony let himself in and announced, "Happy birthday, baby."

"Tony! What are you doing here?"

"I wanted to surprise you."

"I'm...surprised!"

She really was and didn't know what to say. As Laura got hot flashes, she saw everything go up in smoke. Her birthday. Her movie. Her comeback. And most important of all, her relationship with Scott. She should have known Tony would show up to ruin everything since that's what he did best.

Tony glanced around the room. "Looks like you're getting ready to go somewhere. Did you have other plans?"

"Sort of. I was going to meet up with some of the film crew." Laura was so caught off guard, that was all she could come up with.

"Well, call them up and tell them you can't make it," Tony ordered.

Laura nervously looked at her watch again. It was too early for Scott to show up. That would be a complete disaster.

"Where are we going?" she asked.

"I made reservations at a restaurant. We're meeting another couple. It's your birthday! Remember?"

Laura was still in shock that he was even there. "I thought you were filming in Budapest?"

"Yeah, but they stopped production for a few weeks so I could be with you. I planned this all along."

"You're staying?"

Panic set in. This was her worst nightmare. Tony would never leave because she asked him to and he certainly wouldn't leave if she tried to break up with him. That would make things even worse.

Tony asked, "You don't want me here? Sounds like there's a problem."

"No," Laura quickly answered. "Let's go."

Her best bet was to get Tony out of there and deal with him at the restaurant. She didn't want to risk an encounter between Tony and Scott in the hallway. She grabbed her cell phone and followed Tony out the door.

It was a quiet ride in the limo as Laura moved away from Tony every time he got close. Tony could tell something was wrong. Laura knew she was terrible at hiding it.

Finally, Tony asked, "What's going on with you?"

Laura felt cornered. She didn't have an answer. Moreover, she was afraid of Tony and what he would do to her if she told him the truth. Or what he would do to Scott. She saw firsthand what he did to guys he suspected of sleeping with her.

She pulled herself together the best she could and forced a smile.

"I'm so sorry, Tony. It's been a really tough shoot. I'm exhausted."

Tony leaned in for a kiss, but she held her hand up and warned, "And I have my monthly friend."

She was lying, but knew that would back him off a bit and it worked. He simply gave her a peck on the cheek.

Laura just wanted to buy a little time until Tony was gone, but she wasn't sure how long that would be.

When they arrived at the restaurant, a waiter led Tony and Laura to a private table in the VIP section. Already seated was Smooth J, a famous heavy-set rapper. He was accompanied by a gorgeous twenty-something model.

Tony introduced them. "Laura, this is Smooth J."

"The rapper?" she asked.

Smooth J revealed his gold teeth with a smile. "That's me. Happy birthday."

"Thanks," Laura replied, then added, "I thought you were in prison."

Smooth J winked at her. "Just got out."

Tony playfully smacked Laura on the ass as he pulled a chair out for her. They both sat down across from Smooth J and his date.

Tony had some news and wasted no time in telling Laura. "Smooth J and I are going to do a movie together. It's the new thing, you know, to pair rappers up with action stars."

Tony waited for Laura to say something but she just sat there, already uncomfortable. Tony must have felt slightly insulted and raised his voice. "Don't you want to know what it's called?"

Laura stared right through him. Her brain was elsewhere. Her mind was with Scott.

Tony waved his hand in front of her. "Laura?"

She snapped out of it and replied, "Sure, Tony."

"You're going to love this! Tell her J!"

Smooth J looked all around as if what he was about to say was top secret. He whispered, "It's called *Rap Sheet*."

Tony added, "And then J is going to help me lay down some tracks for my rap album."

Even though Laura was in autopilot mode, she heard that and couldn't contain her disgust and talked down to him. "You're recording a rap album? You can't even sing, Tony."

He argued, "I'm learning, baby. That's what Autotune is for."

Smooth J jumped back in. "He gets me in the movies and I'll get him in the rap game."

Laura heard enough and flipped through the menu. She just wanted to eat and get out of there. She drowned out Tony and Smooth J's banter about rap lyrics and tried to come up with a plan. She thought about going to the bathroom and then slipping out the door. Maybe they wouldn't even notice she was gone.

~ * ~

Back at the hotel, Scott strolled through the hallway like he was on top of the world. He was clean-shaven and sported a tie. He hadn't worn a tie since his meeting at the bank. This was a special night for him, and not just because it was Laura's birthday. He had feelings for her that he had never felt before. He had been in his share of various relationships over the years, but this one was different, especially considering how far they came since they met.

He stopped at Laura's door and knocked. He waited. He knocked again and waited some more. He knocked a third time, then pulled out his cell phone and dialed a number. He slumped down in front of the door with the phone to his ear.

~ * ~

Time elapsed at the restaurant and the waiter cleared the table of their plates. Smooth J nodded to Tony just as Laura secretly looked at her cell phone and saw Scott's incoming call.

Smooth J tapped his glass with a fork. "What are you waiting for, Tony?"

Laura wanted to answer her phone. She saw the restrooms nearby. She knew it was time to go and started to stand up, but Smooth J motioned for her to sit back down.

Tony suddenly seemed nervous. He looked Laura right in the eyes and told her, "I wanted to do something extra special for your birthday."

He reached into his jacket and removed a small gift box. Laura's phone stopped ringing just as Tony got down on one knee. He opened the box and revealed an enormous diamond ring.

"Oh no," was all that softly came out of Laura's mouth. She just wanted to disappear and be in Scott's arms, but all she could see was Tony and the diamond ring. She could feel everyone looking at her.

"Laura, will you marry me?" Tony asked.

She always imagined what it would be like when the man of her dreams proposed to her. This wasn't it.

Smooth J clapped as members of the restaurant staff gathered around the table. They also clapped as one of them placed a birthday cake with freshly lit candles on the table.

Laura's hands shook as random staff and onlookers congratulated her. Tony took the diamond ring out of the box and slid it on her finger without even allowing her to answer the proposal. She was overwhelmed and all she wanted to do was get up and run out the door, but she couldn't.

Everyone was singing 'Happy Birthday' to her, so she shifted the attention to her cake and blew out the candles. She sat there expressionless as strangers came up to her and asked to see her ring, asked for an autograph or to pose for pictures. She was completely lost. The hours went by like minutes and the night was over before she knew it.

When Tony and Laura returned to the hotel, she was a zombie. In the hallway, Scott was sound asleep leaned up against Laura's door. She was so out of it, she didn't even notice him, but Tony did and kicked his foot several times. Scott opened his eyes, looked up and saw Tony Steel staring down at him.

"Is this another one of your stalkers?" Tony asked Laura.

Laura snapped out of it and tried to hide behind Tony. She was never more ashamed of herself.

"No, he's part of the film crew. He's fine."

Scott mumbled, "Laura?"

Tony kicked him again. "Beat it!"

Scott stood up and peered around Tony to try to get a glimpse of Laura. She couldn't even look at him and unlocked the door as fast as she could.

All Scott could say was, 'Happy birthday.'

Laura ducked inside while Scott held the gift-wrapped present he brought for her.

Tony angrily asked, "Is that for her? Are you going to give it to her or what?"

Tony snatched it out of his hand. "You were camped out in front of Laura's room." He flexed his arms and cracked his neck. "I should kick your ass just for that."

He lightly smacked Scott on the cheek. "But I'm in a good mood tonight, so I'll pretend it didn't happen. We just got engaged."

Tony slammed the door behind him.

~ * ~

Inside the room, Laura was curled up in a ball on the bed. The engagement ring was already off her finger and sitting on the dresser. She imagined Scott outside her room, perched in a chair, waiting for her to come out, just like always.

Part of her wanted to go out in the hallway and tell Scott she loved him, but she was afraid of what Tony would do to him. She knew all too well how zealously Tony protected his so-called property. She needed Tony to fall asleep so she could leave. Or better yet, she had to break up with him right then and there, but feared for Scott in the hallway. She didn't know what to do. Her birthday curse struck again.

Tony got undressed and tossed Laura the present he took from Scott as he admired his muscles in front of the mirror.

"Open that up right now, cause if it's jewelry, I'm chasing after that punk and teaching him a lesson."

Laura slowly removed the wrapping paper. There was a note on the lid of the box. It read, "I had second thoughts about the name of the bar. I couldn't have done it without you. Love, Scott."

Laura took a deep breath, and opened the lid of the box. She looked inside and pulled out a piece of paper with a drawing on it.

It was an updated sketch of the new exterior of the bar, now with a sign that advertised Laura's Bar and Grill.

Tony was confused and grabbed it out of her hands.

"What the hell is that supposed to mean?" he asked.

After looking at it for a second, he ripped it to shreds and tossed it into the trash. It was more than a piece of paper to Laura. She felt as if Tony had just ripped her heart out and threw it away.

~ * ~

Indeed, Scott did wait in the hallway, but not for nearly as long as Laura thought. In his mind, she could have walked out of that room and left with him, but she chose not to. That's what hurt the most. He remembered the rose he had brought Laura on his first night as her bodyguard, when she ripped the bud from the stem and stomped on it with her foot. He felt like that rose.

While Scott knew he was no match for Tony Steel, he didn't care. If Laura walked out and chose him, he was ready to accept whatever punishment Tony inflicted on him. More importantly, he intended to protect Laura from Tony, but it didn't matter. She never came out. As much as it hurt him to do so, Scott gave up and went on his way and headed to the bar.

Once there, he stepped around all the wires and camera equipment in the dark. He turned on a light that revealed the *Pretty Ugly* movie set.

He walked over to a booth where an elaborate surprise waited for Laura. There was a fancy dinner, unlit candles on a birthday cake and balloons everywhere.

Scott was normally a calm person, but on this night, he let his frustration get the best of him. He knocked the plates off the table and they shattered on the floor. Then he threw the birthday cake across the room where it splattered on the wall. He looked around at the bar that would soon be his. It wasn't even worth it now.

After he sat down for a while and cooled off, Scott cleaned up his mess and locked the bar back up behind him. At home, he just stayed in bed and stared at the ceiling. He didn't know how he got to this point. He couldn't even stand Laura when they met and now his stomach was in knots over her.

In the morning, Scott was still wide-awake when the doorbell rang. He looked out the window and saw a limousine parked in the driveway and got excited. Seconds later, Scott opened the front door, only to see Tony Steel again.

"Scott?" Tony asked.

"Hey," Scott sighed, as he realized Laura was nowhere in sight.

Tony seemed somewhat friendly and unusually soft-spoken. "About last night, I didn't realize you were Laura's bodyguard. Nobody tells me anything."

Tony pointed to the limo. "Laura and I would like to take you out for breakfast."

Scott wasn't interested. "No, thanks. I think I'm going to pass."

Tony continued, "Laura insists. She asked me to come get you."

Scott thought for a moment. Was Laura in the limo or was it some kind of trap? Either way, he needed to face off with Tony sooner or later. If Laura was in the limo, he intended to fight for her.

Scott said, "Sure. Why not?"

He closed the door and followed Tony to the limousine. He climbed inside and the limo quickly drove away. Inside, Scott found himself sitting across from only Tony Steel and Smooth J.

"So where's Laura?" Scott asked.

Tony struggled to sit still as he clenched a magazine. Smooth J calmly puffed on a cigar. There was a long silence before Tony finally asked, "Do you know why I'm really here?"

Scott replied, "We're not having breakfast with Laura, are we?"

Tony laughed. "No."

Scott did his best to stay calm. He saw enough Jimmy Corn gangster movies to know that these types of rides did not end well. Were they going to throw him in the river? Feed him to a lion in somebody's basement? Or bury him alive? Luckily for Scott, they were nowhere near a desert.

"Where are we going?" Scott asked.

Tony looked at the cover of the magazine in his hand.

"Scott, do you read Celebrity Weekly magazine?"

"No. That's not my thing. I know what it is though."

Tony continued, "In this business, you have to read it. You never know when the paparazzi are watching. You know what I mean?"

Tony held up the magazine for Scott to see, turned to a specific page and threw it on his lap.

"I got a call this week telling me to pick it up."

Scott looked down at the magazine and a chill came over him. There was a very clear picture of Scott and Laura kissing while they danced at the restaurant.

Scott was busted, but he didn't care. He was in love with Laura and wanted Tony to know it, regardless of the consequence. Scott simply shrugged his shoulders and announced, "You don't deserve Laura."

Smooth J blew a puff of smoke in his face while Tony stared him down. Tony pulled out his cell phone and dialed a number. He waited until someone answered on the other end and then simply said, "Do it." Tony laughed as he hung up the phone.

Tony glared at Scott and said, "You want to know what I just did?"

Scott feared the worst. He didn't want any harm to come to Laura because of him. Scott begged, "Please don't hurt Laura. This is my fault. Do whatever you want to me. Just leave her out of it."

"Too late," Tony replied. Smooth J tapped on the inside window to get the attention of the driver.

Seconds later, the limousine pulled over into a dark alley and parked in a corner. Smooth J jumped out and held the door open. Tony followed and forcibly drug Scott out with him and threw him to the ground.

Scott climbed back to his feet and got one good punch on Tony's chin, but it barely fazed him. Scott didn't care if he landed any more punches; he enjoyed getting that one shot in. Scott was going to savor that right hook for the rest of his life.

Tony pushed Scott back down and asked, "Is that all you got?"

Tony and Smooth J took turns punching and kicking Scott. He spit up blood and tried to crawl away from them several times, but they pulled him back and kicked him some more.

Scott had been in his fair share of brawls from working at the bar, but he was no match for Tony. This was the first time in his life he was ever severely beaten. He felt every punch and kick down to his bones. His vision blurred and his ears started to ring. He knew he was about to go unconscious but was determined to stay awake.

Smooth J pulled Tony away. "Let's go, Tony. He's had enough. We're not in LA."

Tony launched one more punch before walking away from him.

Scott mounted enough strength to prop himself up. As he wobbled on his feet, he sternly said, "Your movies suck!"

Tony rushed back in with a roundhouse kick, knocking Scott unconscious. Tony and Smooth J jumped in the limo and sped off.

~ * ~

Later that morning on the movie set, Victor was trying to calm Jimmy down while Matt and his entourage were huddled around a laptop.

With all the grunts and moans, it sounded like they were watching internet porn.

Jimmy screamed, "Turn it off!"

Matt closed the laptop and led his entourage outside.

Victor explained, "Jimmy, just calm down. We can spin this in our favor. We'll make it work."

As Jimmy paced around the set, crew members scrambled to avoid bumping into him or making eye contact. Without warning, Jimmy made a break for the door. He knew exactly what he had to do. Nobody attempted to chase after him, not even Victor.

~ * ~

Laura rode in the backseat of the car while her mother drove. When they pulled into the parking lot of the bar, they could see photographers scattered everywhere.

"Oh my god, Mom, I'm ruined."

"Let me handle this dear. Stay here."

Once Sophia got out of the car and went inside the bar, the photographers immediately swarmed the passenger side of the vehicle. In between the blinding lights of the cameras, Laura saw Matt and his entourage join in with the photographers. She didn't care about him though. She was only interested in seeing if Scott was somewhere out there.

They all started to bang on the windows and call out her name. Matt made obscene gestures and pretended to hump the hood. He pushed the photographers out of his way and pressed his face up against her window. Laura looked right at him and held up her middle finger between his eyes. This seemed to infuriate Matt and he unbuckled his pants and pressed his bare ass against the window. The photographers continued to take pictures.

Once Sophia returned to the car, Matt backed away, but continued to laugh with his friends. As Sophia quickly drove off, Laura turned and looked back. She saw Jimmy grab a camera from one of the photographers and smash it to pieces. He chased after their car, swinging his arms in the air like a lunatic. She kept hoping for one last glimpse of Scott, but never got one as the car got farther away and the bar slowly disappeared from her view.

CHAPTER FOURTEEN
Rock Bottom

Jimmy arrived at the hotel with a crazed look in his eye. He walked briskly through the hotel lobby and took the elevators to Laura's floor. He stopped at her door and kicked it while he screamed, "Tony Steel?! Are you in there?!"

Moments later, the door swung open and Jimmy let himself in. Tony closed the door behind them.

"Jimmy Corn!" Tony exclaimed.

"Tony Steel!" Jimmy returned.

Smooth J was eating a bag of potato chips on the sofa. He held the bag out to Jimmy, offering him some, but Jimmy smacked it into the air, covering Smooth J and the sofa with potato chips.

Smooth J took offense. "Hey man! What's your problem?!"

"I need to talk to Tony! Alone!"

Smooth J looked to Tony, who gave a nod of approval. Smooth J grabbed his jacket and left the room.

Tony laughed and said, "So...Jimmy Crack Corn. What brings you here?"

'What did you call me?" Jimmy asked.

Tony moved closer to him. "Jimmy Crack Corn...and I don't care. Isn't that how it goes?"

At this point, Tony was pouring gasoline on the fire. Jimmy circled him like a shark and said, "I haven't been called that since I was a kid."

Tony seemed to sense the threat and tried to diffuse him. "Jimmy! Do you have any idea what's happening on your movie set? When are we going to team up and make the action film your fans really want?"

Jimmy started to shake and clenched his pocket like he was reaching for something.

Tony continued his attack. "And what's up with this cheesy love story? Are you going soft on us? A chick flick? What happened to you?"

Jimmy pulled his Chinese star out of his pocket and threw it right at him. It lodged right into the center of Tony's forehead.

Tony appeared to be in complete shock. He felt the Chinese star sticking out of his forehead and tried to pull it out, but it was stuck in there pretty good. Jimmy was impressed with his own precision.

This was supposed to be Jimmy's comeback and he was prepared to forever blame Tony Steel if the movie was a flop. Jimmy needed a scapegoat, now he had one. He watched as a trickle of blood dripped from the wound and down the bridge of Tony's nose.

Jimmy informed Tony of the blame. "You ruined my romantic comedy, Tony Steel!"

Tony Steel, the once macho action star, danced around while tapping the Chinese star with his fingers, afraid to touch it too hard. He burst into tears as he reached for a phone and dialed 911.

Jimmy calmly walked by him and out the door.

Minutes later, police cars and ambulances surrounded the front entrance of the hotel. Jimmy waited outside with his hands in the air, ready to surrender to police. It was worth it to him though. Tony Steel was wheeled out the door on a stretcher. He was sobbing uncontrollably as the Chinese star protruded from his forehead.

He was placed into an ambulance while Jimmy Corn enjoyed the view from the backseat of a police car. Jimmy had no real criminal history, so he didn't expect to do any hardcore jail time, just maybe a stretch of house arrest in Hollywood.

~ * ~

Over at Victor's Bar and Grill, Scott limped across the parking lot. He noticed that the film crew was dismantling equipment and loading it into a truck.

Scott entered the bar to find that most of the evidence of the movie shoot was gone. The only people still hanging around were Dennis and Victor.

Victor took one look at Scott's beaten face and hung his head in shame. Dennis rushed to his side. "Scott, are you all right?"

Scott wasn't the least bit concerned about his injuries. "I'll be fine. Where's Laura?"

Victor told him, "She's taking the next flight to LA with her mother. It's for the best. She needs to lay low for a little while until things calm down."

Scott wanted answers. "I don't understand. What happened?"

Dennis asked, "You didn't hear?"

Victor quickly cleared things up. "Laura broke up with Tony in her hotel room last night. Apparently, she told him she was in love with someone else. Tony retaliated this morning by releasing a sex tape of Laura. It's all over the internet."

Scott was overloaded with conflicting emotions: anger and sadness for Laura, disgust and hatred for Tony, and shame and pity for himself. This was easily the worst day of his life. On top of being physically beaten down, both on the inside and out, he was mad at himself for not standing up to Tony Steel the night before and he didn't understand why Laura didn't seek him out before leaving for Los Angeles. He knew he was the one she referenced about being in love, but why would she say something like that and not even say goodbye?

Victor took the moment to hand him a check. Scott looked at it and immediately questioned the amount. "This is more than we agreed on. A lot more."

Victor apologized. "I'm sorry, kid. I feel terrible about this whole thing. For what Tony did. For getting you mixed up with Laura."

Scott interrupted. "No, don't say that."

The last few weeks with Laura were some of the best of his life. He made memories with her that he would never forget. Victor couldn't possibly understand. Nobody could. And how dare he apologize for introducing him to Laura.

Victor simply added, "It's to hopefully make up for all your troubles."

Dennis tossed Scott a key. "Here's my key. I won't need it anymore. You can open up tomorrow. It's all yours now."

Scott dreamed of this moment for years, but now that the key was in his hand, he knew he would trade it for Laura in an instant. He felt lost.

"I don't know. It just doesn't feel the same."

Dennis was confused and simply said, "This is what you've been waiting for."

He heard Dennis, but was uninterested in that conversation. Instead, he asked Victor, "Did Laura happen to say anything?"

"About what?"

"About me!"

"No. Why?"

Victor seemed clueless about their relationship. After all, they hid it well.

This caught Scott completely off guard. He would have expected something like this from the old Laura, but not the Laura he fell in love with. He glanced around in vain, hoping there was an envelope taped to something with his name on it. She had to have left some kind of message with someone.

Scott asked, "What about the rest of the movie shoot? She's not coming back?"

Victor didn't seem too concerned or upset, as if he already had a plan. "No. We're going to shoot the rest in LA. We'll rebuild the set from scratch if we have to. No one will know the difference, except maybe Jimmy."

Victor shook Scott's hand. "Once again, my apologies."

Victor turned to Dennis. "Thanks for everything, Dennis."

He took one last look around the bar and walked out. He was honestly just glad to be going back to LA. Scott clenched the key in his hand and looked at Victor's portrait on the wall. Dennis handed Scott a rag and he wiped the blood from his face. Scott sat down at the bar and Dennis joined him. They talked that night for hours, more than they had in years. Scott told him everything about his secret relationship with Laura and how they hated each other before falling in love. Then Dennis shared his own life experiences in both good and bad relationships. He told Scott stories he'd never told anyone else. He even made Scott laugh a few times. By the end of the night his heart was still broken, but Dennis helped ease his pain, even if only just a little bit.

Scott didn't know how he could ever accept that Laura was gone. He felt like she took his heart with her on the plane to Los Angeles. He second-guessed every decision he made in the last twenty-four hours. What could he have done different that would have kept Laura by his side?

Scott didn't sleep that night. He just waited for his phone to ring. Maybe she would call in the morning? Or the next day? Or after a week? Every time his phone rang it was torture. His heart always skipped a beat with the possibility that it was Laura. But she never called.

CHAPTER FIFTEEN
Last Chance

Six months later...

Scott was among the sold-out crowd leaving the movie theater. The marquee read, *Love Me Do*. He stopped by the poster that was hanging near the box office. Laura and Matt were front and center. He stared into Laura's eyes and for a moment it seemed like she was looking back at him. Finally, he turned away and walked down the street. As much as he had tried to move on from Laura, he just had to see the movie and see her, because in a way, it was their movie.

~ * ~

Across the country in Hollywood, Victor sat at his desk and flipped through the entertainment section of a newspaper. A closer look at the article revealed the headline, '*Love Me Do* Crosses Hundred Million Dollar Mark. Sequel in the Works.' Victor was back on top and celebrated with a cigar.

~ * ~

At the Summer mansion in Beverly Hills, Laura climbed out of bed and grabbed a script off the towering pile stacked in her room. She opened it up and started reading. She suddenly found herself on the A-list again and struggling to keep track of all the offers coming in through Sophia.

~ * ~

In a recording studio, Tony Steel spit rhymes into a microphone while Smooth J ran the control board. The scar on Tony's forehead was a faint reminder of the Chinese star. Tony loved to hear himself sing and was excited for the world to hear his debut rap album.

~ * ~

In his office, Jimmy opened a scriptwriting program on his computer. With a blank page in front of him, he typed the title, *Love Me Do 2*. He thought for a moment, backspaced over the title and typed, *Love Me Two Times*, written by Jimmy Corn. With the unexpected success of the film, Jimmy had a newfound respect for romantic comedies and wasn't sure when he would return to bloody action films...for now.

~ * ~

Back in Pennsylvania, a brand new neon sign advertised Laura's Bar and Grill. It flickered for a second before turning off. Moments later, Scott stepped out of the bar with Ricky and Alison and locked the door behind them.

Scott said, "The bride and groom are going to be late."

Ricky argued, "It's just our rehearsal, not the actual wedding."

Ricky stopped and kissed Alison who added, "I can't believe we're getting married tomorrow."

They all climbed into Scott's car and headed into town. When they arrived at the church, friends and family greeted them, but none of the Summers were there.

Alison and Ricky stood before the reverend. On each side of them were the bridesmaids and the groomsmen, including Scott.

The reverend counted those in attendance. He asked, "Who's missing from the bridal party?"

Ricky informed him, "My sister is a bridesmaid. She's on a movie shoot. She's flying in overnight with the rest of my family."

"Laura Summer?" asked the reverend.

Alison smiled. "She's sort of the one that introduced us."

The reverend was slightly concerned. "I just don't want her to be confused or lost during the actual ceremony."

Ricky assured him, "She once did a movie about a wedding, so we figure she'll do all right."

The reverend laughed it off. "Okay, but you'll have to introduce me to her tomorrow. I would love to meet her. And maybe even get a picture."

Scott wanted to say something, but he held it in. This was an awkward situation for him. He was happy for his sister and Ricky, but they were a constant reminder of his failed relationship with Laura. And of course, part of him was jealous, too. This could have been him getting married. Just when he felt like he was finally getting over Laura, he had to take the double punch of her movie being released and the pressure of seeing her for the first time at the wedding. He prepared himself all these months for what he would say to Laura whenever he saw her again, but he was going to be nervous no matter what.

The reverend asked Ricky, "May I have the vows you prepared?"

Ricky patted himself down and checked all his pockets. He panicked as he turned to Scott and said, "They're written on a piece of paper I left at the bar, right where I was sitting. Can you run and get it?"

Scott couldn't believe it and asked, "Seriously?" He chalked it up as another Ricky Summer goof and sighed, "Yeah, sure, no problem."

Alison jumped in, "Thanks, Scott."

Scott joked, "Need anything else while I'm out?"

Ricky sensed the sarcasm. "No. Just the vows, please. Thanks!"

When Scott arrived at the bar, everything was dark. There were signs all over the place congratulating Ricky and Alison. After unlocking the door, he turned on just one small lamp at the bar so he could find the piece of paper with the vows written on it. He saw a piece of paper next to a beer mug. That had to be it.

He picked it up and looked at it. He wasn't really interested in reading their vows, but wanted to make sure he had the right thing. A closer look at the piece of paper revealed certain letters written across the page: A, E, I, O and U.

Scott found it somewhat amusing and mumbled to himself, "Really, Ricky?"

There was one more piece of paper underneath it. He picked that one up. It was tattered and stitched together with scotch tape. It was the sketch of the exterior of the bar with the Laura's Bar and Grill sign, the one that he gave to Tony Steel in the hotel hallway for Laura's birthday.

~ * ~

Laura waited outside the bar and watched Scott through the window. She saw him pick up the sketch and knew that was her cue. She was purposely wearing the same red cocktail dress she wore the night she arrived in town, the first night they met. She nervously ran her hand through her hair, took a deep breath and made her entrance into the bar.

Scott instinctively said, "Sorry, we're closed," as he looked up to see who walked into the bar. Laura stood there for a moment and let it sink in. Scott appeared surprised, like he saw a ghost.

Laura was hypnotized at the sight of Scott. She felt a sudden rush of blood run through her entire body while butterflies bounced around in her stomach. She felt like she could faint at any moment. She had so many things to say, but nothing came out.

Finally, she managed to simply say, "Hi."

"Hi," Scott predictably replied.

"Are you open?" was all Laura could think of.

Scott held up the piece of paper with the letters. "Ricky said he forgot his vows."

Laura confessed, "Yeah, that was my idea. He has the real ones."

"So I guess they don't need me back at the church?"

"No. I put him up to it. I wanted to see the place. You named it after me."

"Yes I did." They both looked at the picture of Laura on the wall where Victor's portrait used to hang. They glanced back and forth at each other as Laura slowly made her way to Scott.

Laura clarified, "And I wanted to see you."

Once Laura reached the bar and they were face to face, she started to cry. She didn't try to fight it, and let the tears fall.

Scott did what he did best and immediately tried to comfort her with words. "Congrats on the movie. I heard it might get some nominations."

Laura was genuinely surprised. "You saw it?"

"Of course."

"You know, I couldn't have done it without you. Remember how you told me to think of something bad that happened to me for my big crying scene?"

Scott asked, "It worked?"

Laura cried a little harder.

That was the last thing Scott wanted to happen. "What's the matter?" he quickly asked.

Laura added, "I thought about what I did to you...and how much I hurt you."

Scott reached across the bar and wiped the tears away.

Laura explained, "When I filmed that scene, I didn't see Matt. I saw you. I even changed my lines. Jimmy loved it and that's the take he used."

"You did a great job in the movie. You were amazing."

Laura touched the old, rickety bar stool next to her that had all the initials carved into it. Scott reached under the counter and pulled out a small knife, placed it on the bar and slid it over to her. He pointed to the bar stool.

"Being that the place is named after you, I think it's only fair."

Laura took the knife and carefully carved the letters L and S underneath Scott's initials, S and S. She then took it one step further and enclosed their initials with a heart as if it was an old oak tree.

As Scott admired her work, he finally asked Laura the tough question she knew was coming. "Why didn't you call?"

No matter how prepared she was to answer him, there was nothing she could say that would excuse her silence all this time. All she could do was string a bunch of words together. "I could go on about Tony, the tape, rehab, my mom, my dad, but there's no excuse. They told me Tony hurt you. I should have reached out somehow, but I was ashamed. And after the tape came out, I didn't know what you thought of me. I was a mess."

Some more tears ran down Laura's face, but Scott wiped them away. Laura collected her thoughts, looked Scott right in the eye and said, "I'm so sorry for what I did to you. I didn't want us to end. You made me so happy."

"You were the best thing to ever happen to me," Scott countered.

Laura seductively whispered, "I have missed you so much."

Scott admitted, "I've missed you too."

Laura composed herself, smiled and cut right to the chase. "I have a huge favor to ask of you."

"Sure. Anything," Scott said.

The ice was completely broken. It was almost as if the events that led up to this moment had never happened.

Laura could barely contain her excitement. "I'm filming a movie in Ocean City, New Jersey, and really need someone to follow me around and keep me out of trouble. Would you be interested?"

Scott appeared torn. "I own a bar now. It's not that easy to just go away like that."

"No problem. Ricky and your sister said they would handle everything while you're gone. And then I thought maybe, when the movie's done, I could return the favor and follow you around a little bit, and help you out at the bar. That is, if you want me to."

Scott warned her up front. "I can be hard to please."

"I'm willing to put up with you. I mean, you had to put up with me."

"But bartending is a real job. No limo. No craft services. No agent. Just a day's work."

Scott tossed a washcloth at her and added, "Why don't you come over to this side of the bar and do your research?"

Laura played along. "I don't want to mess up my manicure."

Laura set her phone on the bar and opened up her music app. She located a song and hit play. It was their song. The song they danced to when they first kissed.

Laura smiled and asked, "May I have this dance?"

She walked around and joined Scott on his side of the bar and wrapped her arms around him. She couldn't get over how good that felt and realized how much she truly had missed him.

They danced, kissed, smiled and laughed until the song came to an end. Scott didn't want to let Laura go but she slipped away from him and hurried back to the other side of the bar. She looked through some more music on her phone.

"I brought another song with me too."

She hit play and waited for a response from Scott. He appeared stunned as he immediately recognized it as the theme song from *My Little Robot*.

Laura started to make bizarre mechanical moves with her arms and legs. She gave Scott a private performance of the robot dance that normally would have been awkward and humorous, but the way she looked at Scott turned it into something completely unexpected. She made the robot dance sexy.

When the song was over, Scott clapped and she bowed. She walked toward the bar with her usual strut but with a different attitude. She was finally comfortable with herself and ready to start over and give their relationship a real chance.

As she approached Scott, he reached his hand out and gently touched her face as she closed her eyes. He planted a soft kiss on her lips and said, "Thank you for showing me that."

That was too gentle for Laura, so she grabbed Scott by his shirt and pulled him across the bar. Her glass of water shattered. Her cell phone fell to the floor, but she didn't care. Once his feet were stable, she wrapped her legs around him and passionately kissed him. Somehow, one of Ricky and Alison's wedding signs came down and flew between them and onto the floor.

Random stools fell over as their bodies ricocheted around the room with their lips locked. Laura could hear Scott's heavy breathing and it turned her on. She didn't care where they did it. On the bar, the floor, the pool table, anywhere.

When they got closer to the lamp, Scott stretched his arm and turned it off. The bar went completely dark. Laura continued to kiss him for a moment, but then pulled herself away and turned the light back on.

Laura took a few steps back and slipped out of her red dress. She was completely naked and draped the dress over the broken barstool, right next to their initials.

As Laura stepped directly into the light, she knew what she had to say. It was time.

She whispered, "I love you."

~ THE END ~

Coming Soon:
My Little Bridesmaid

The story picks up right where we left off and continues with Scott and Laura's wild weekend at Ricky and Alison's wedding. Subscribe to the newsletter to be the first to read it!

MORE FROM THE AUTHOR

My Little Trainwreck
is the first book in the Laura Summer Series!
Subscribe to the newsletter to receive news on
upcoming books in the series, as well as sneak
peeks, free book downloads and bonus
chapters only available to subscribers!
www.mylittletrainwreck.com/newsletter.html

Please leave an honest review of this book on
its Amazon page!

The Book's Website
www.mylittletrainwreck.com
www.facebook.com/mylittletrainwreck

Author's Website
www.ericmoyer.com

Author's Twitter
www.twitter.com/moyereric

Author's Instagram
www.instagram.com/backtooceancity

Scott's YouTube Cat
www.wilberthecat.com

Email the Author
eric@moyermovies.com

Download the author's first book:
Back to Ocean City:
A Screenwriter's Journey
featuring the original movie script for
My Little Trainwreck.
www.amazon.com/gp/product/B00X3C7348
www.backtooceancity.com
www.facebook.com/backtooceancity